Where the River Bends and Curls

Paul John Hausleben

The cover design is by Paul John Hausleben
The photograph of the author is by Ms. Alejandra Lopez
All artwork and logos are by Paul John Hausleben

Published by God Bless the Keg Publishing
Somewhere, U.S.A.

ISBN: 978-0-9906979-1-6

Dedication

To the memories of what we have shared in life and to all the fresh memories that we continue to create.

Where the River Bends and Curls

Paul John Hausleben

Contents

Acknowledgements

Thank you, as always, to Mr. Harry M. Rogers Junior. Thank you to my old trout-fishing pal and stream companion, Mr. Andrew Lord. Thank you to my friends and family and the young couple on the plane. Thank you to Caryss for allowing me to steal a heartfelt blurb for the perfect spot in the storyline. Thanks for the inspiration, to the sound of those quiet ripples of a trout stream early in the morning, right before the sun appears in the sky. Most of all, thank you for allowing me to recall the wonderful sparkle in her eyes.

"I am here, and I will always be here. I might become a dusty, old memory for you, but on your darkest days, you will always be able to recall your fondest memories."

Paul John Hausleben

September 2015

Preface from the Author

This novel, as my material often does, came into fruition because of a touch of rather spontaneous and unanticipated inspiration. In the early part of the year 2015, on an airplane flight on one of my many ventures, I was sitting in the aisle seat on a flight from West Palm Beach, Florida, to return to my home up north. The flight was carrying me home after I had completed a successful business trip; however, it was a bit of a mindless mission, and I have to admit that I was suffering from a severe case of the doldrums. I also was in a bit of a creative lull. I had my hockey novel, *Geyer Street Gardens* into the final scrubs and edits and that was a project, of which I was happy, finally to complete. It had taken me about three years to finish, and I swear that novel had aged me a bit.

Perhaps, it was a bit of writer's intuition of an upcoming project, but I snuck into the storyline of *Geyer Street Gardens* a hint of a past romance for the character of Paul John Henson. In one of his many remembrances, Henson briefly mentions, and recalls, the name of a certain young woman with whom he had a past romantic involvement with a long time ago. It was a recollection that until this particular point in his narratives, the character never previously mentioned or even hinted at, and certainly, for followers of the past adventures, it will be a surprise to hear of a new encounter in Henson's usually, humdrum romantic past.

I am often amazed at how these mysterious thoughts and spurious inspirations all eventually interlock to become stories.

Speaking to a close friend over a few beers just a week or so earlier than my trip to Florida, I casually mentioned how

I would not start any new writing projects. I wanted to work on and perfect what I already had in draft, and perhaps concentrate on some other ideas. My goal was to do some audio and video work, increase my marketing and improve part of my writing infrastructure. I had recently decided to use different software to write with, and the complexity of learning the new product, and trying hard to forget my old software habits, proved a bit more daunting than I originally imagined. The software was, however, a pleasant diversion to keep me off the street corners and out of the local gin mills.

The last project I wanted to begin right at this moment would be a novel, novelette, or a novella. I could handle some material in and around five thousand words, no more, perhaps less. The cows were beyond milking. The inspiration well was a bit dry; I needed to concentrate on what I had in the works and not begin anything new.

I am quite fortunate in that I rarely suffer from a writer's block, I can always write something, but at times, the inspiration is weak, and the quality of what I am composing does not make the cut. This was one of those times. I had many volumes of work in progress, but I currently felt it was too weak and uninspired to pursue.

Then along came that bloomin' airplane flight.

Please, Hausleben, never say that you will never do something.

I sat in the aisle seat of a row, with a young couple occupying the middle seat and window seat of the same aisle. After exchanging some of the usual casual greetings and mindless pleasantries, we were sitting in silence until about an hour or so into the flight, when we hit a bit of turbulence, and the young couple held hands in a display of affection, and of profound nervousness. They appeared to be nervous fliers.

Ah, hah! That observation stuck in my eccentric mind as inspirational thought number one for the day; young love and innocence revealed to my mental notebook.

I leaned in and advised them as an old hand on airline flights that this was perfectly normal. After they calmed down, and the airplane stopped leaping and bouncing, and they realized that I was correct, we struck up more of an in-depth conversation. It turns out that this fine-looking couple happened to be two university students, a boyfriend and girlfriend, returning to their university located in my home state, after a holiday for their spring break in Florida. Not just a run-of-the-mill university, but also a shall-remain unnamed, expensive and very exclusive university!

Oh my, a bit different from my educational background for sure; however, I will never discount or belittle my "diplomas" that I earned on the fun-filled streets of Paterson and Haledon, New Jersey.

The young woman was quite a gorgeous woman. I would even label her a stunning beauty. She was majoring her studies in German, and she told me that she might become a teacher, or perhaps the language might just come in handy for traveling the world. Okay, now be nice, Hausleben! Try hard to skip comment on that one here, Hausleben; resist your usual humor and eccentric mannerisms, but I thought, 'It must be nice to have such troubles.' The young man was studying English. Ah, hah! Here was the inspirational factor number two.

Inevitably, the two of them asked as to what I did to earn a few extra baubles and trinkets to stow in my sporran.

I told them that I was a storyteller.

The young man's eyes perked up; his curiosity peaked now. He asked, "As in that is all you do, is to tell stories or do you write them down?"

"No, I tell stories by writing them down."

"You are an author then?"

"No, a storyteller. Calling me an author is a bit of a stretch. I prefer to be known as a storyteller that uses words on printed paper or whiz-bang electronic whoosies to tell my stories."

He leaned back, totally confused, most likely deciding that I was just an eccentric weirdo. In the meantime, the young woman, after she stopped laughing, asked for my name. I gave her one of my business cards and she was now on the big search engine in the sky, literally, and soon she found me. After viewing what is now quite an extensive volume of poppycock that I have composed over the years, it fascinated the young man. He proceeded to ask me about a million and one questions.

"Do you ever get writer's block? Where do you receive inspiration? What do you write? How have you written so many books and stories in such a short period? Where do you find characters to create? Why do you write?" And so on and so forth.

I answered them all. He was quite energetic, pleasant and obviously extremely intelligent. He then sadly lamented how he goofed off on spring break, chased the young lady around playing grab-ass with her a bit too much, and now he had to write a short story before returning to class. He only had one remaining day to complete it and he had no idea on what he would write about for the story. No characters, no storyline, no theme . . . nothing. He had a pad and pen in his hand, with nothing written down on his pad.

At first, I did not comment, and after the conversation died down a bit and I watched him sadly float his pen over the pad for about fifteen minutes and not write a bloody word down, I asked him if I could borrow his pad and pen.

Puzzled, he handed it to me, and I wrote down, "A young writer meets an experienced, yet eccentric storyteller on an airplane ride."

I handed the pad and pen back to him and watched as the smile broke out on his face. His gal leaned in, read what I wrote down on the pad. She laughed and gently grabbed my arm.

She gave me a brief but heartfelt kiss on the cheek, while telling me, "Thank you. He was being a major pain in my gorgeous ass and he was really getting on my damn last nerve! I am Jewish and he is Catholic, so we make an odd couple to begin with! Plus, you are a very good-looking man. I have to say that I love the beard too. Besides, you have a fun personality. Maybe we can talk and smooch a little more and I can make him jealous!"

She gave me a little wink. Ah, hah! Here are the pieces of inspiration number three, with a sharp-tongued, self-confident, gorgeous, young woman. She is involved in a mixed-religion relationship, proceeds to flirt a bit, share some of her allure and a little harmless kiss with me, and pass along a compliment or two.

All this from a stranger who also is a lovely young woman.

What an awesome character to create! Now, my wheels were turning and the creative meter bounced a bit.

The airplane landed. We exchanged goodbyes, "Have an enjoyable life" type of banter that you usually exchange with people whom you assume you will never see again during the rest of your lifetime, and our chance meeting was over.

On the other hand, was it?

You can imagine my surprise when about three weeks later; I received an email from the same young man with a document attached to the message. The document turned out to be a character study. A paper, which was obviously an assignment for a course requirement, and a paper the young man composed for submitting towards that same course requirement. The character that the young student studied for the paper was my own character, "Paul John Henson" from the Adventures of Harry and Paul!

Imagine that, a character of mine, studied, analyzed and then submitted in a study to a university professor. How this life is full of twists and turns. I must say the realization of how profound this all was brought a tear or two into this battle-hardened storyteller's eyes.

The character study of Mr. Henson was extremely in-depth, very comprehensive, and quite complex. However, after reading the entire document and summarizing the young student's focal points, I combined it with the previous inspiration received from the young couple and found what I required to inspire the rest of the basis of *Where the River Bends and Curls.*

It was certainly an aspect of life, which I admit that I found fascinating, that a person could decipher this and probe deep inside my mind to pull together a study of a fictional character that I created! I do think his study was dead on, so much so that it sends some shivers up and down my spine!

The document is extensive and I feel that sharing more than just the focal points here would be a mistake. I think that each reader has to interpret the characters on their own, in their own way, see them through their own eyes. However, I will share that this reader determined that Mr. Henson is an incredible romantic; in addition, he is a severely conflicted man, a reluctant, but dedicated religious leader, a fearless person and an incessant dreamer who is forever lost in the past. The rest of the study. . ..

My, oh my, did that set the wheels rolling on the old inspirational train. Despite my vow not to begin an additional work, this novel was now born! Fueled by a bit of a fine, single malt Scotch that I gave to myself as a Christmas gift, I feverishly set to work and wrote the draft version of this book within three days of very intense writing.

This book is, by far, the boldest to date that I have ever written. It is slightly sexual, with an extensive smattering of obscenities and other authentic language. *Where the River Bends and Curls* is a novel that contains a large amount of flowery romance and emotions, it is intense and different, and much as the character study is, it is an in-depth view into Paul John Henson, without the influences of the other characters.

In and amongst these pages you will find Harry M. Redmond Junior and Jeff Porter, Binky Hobnobber Henson, the old man, and some other characters from the *Adventures of Harry and Paul*, but for the first time, they do so, as minor characters. Hence, this is not an adventure of the boyhood friends, with the character of Harry M. Redmond Junior being the bombastic star, and Mr. Henson being Harry's faithful sidekick and life coach, but this time around, this book is an unfamiliar vehicle.

I even dug around deeply in the story vault to find an old storyline out of one of the old novels, to tie some of Mr. Henson's past life up in a golden memory, in order to fit the hopeless romantic inspiration that I had received.

Yes, this novel is very different and sometimes, in this life, you do need to step out of your comfort zone. Acknowledgement of that fact is somewhat frightening but rewarding too. It was time to break the old mold and see what comes out of a new one. *Where the River Bends and Curls* is a novel that required more roundabout inspiration in order to compose than my previous work and it now has a long-winded history. That is my comfort zone. It often takes me a long time to compile what I need to put some of this drivel together, and for me, that part of the mission is a rather enjoyable experience.

I enjoyed writing this novel, and I hope that you enjoy reading this book as much as I enjoyed the experience of writing it.

Thank you for reading it.

Paul John Hausleben
September 2015

Prologue

I sensed that my wife had finally lost patience with me as my lovely Binky rather forcibly instructed me, "My dear Paul, today, would you please, please, please, go through those boxes that I pulled out of the storage closet in the basement? Please throw away what is junk, or if it is something which is still good, but you do not want any longer, we can place it in the donation boxes for church."

I knew that Binky meant business, because while she spoke, she also jammed her foot into the ground as she often did to emphasize a point. She also stood in the center of the kitchen, pointed at the basement door, and then she folded her arms across her ample breasts and fumed a bit at me. In fairness, I deserved the stern direction from Binky. She was asking me for what I do think was the second or perhaps, even the third or fourth time, to perform a cleanup mission of my "stuff." I had put it off for too long and now there was no escape. I needed to shake my doodle or face her wrath. Time to begin doodle shaking, there twenty-seven!

Admittedly, this was not exactly what I wanted to do, nor what I had in mind, for this particular Saturday afternoon. I had a paper to write for work, and the hockey playoffs were on in about two hours.

Excuses, more specifically, lame excuses, but nonetheless, they were excuses, of which I was happy to conjure up in order to justify putting off other duties. This was not my usual behavior; I usually was cooperative and took my duties and household missions very seriously. I never shirked my work, assignments, or duties. I could not put my finger on why, as of late, I just could not become motivated. To be honest, I had recently fallen into some sort of deep funk, the doldrums, and a profound and deep weariness was gradually creeping into my body and into my soul. I had no immediate cure for this, and now it was of some concern to me.

I was not sure what was happening to me. Was it a touch of depression? Was it my health? Here I was, a Lutheran pastor. In fact, I was now serving my district as a bishop, professionally trained in counseling people, and I could not recognize my own ills.

It was very disturbing to me.

Recently, I had nagging thoughts that I felt were very strange, unusual and inexplicable. Oddly, they included profound thoughts of a past, passionate relationship, a lost love, a wonderful woman that I met long before I even knew Binky. For some unknown reason, as of late, I could not shake these strange thoughts. It was eating away at me, and I prayed fervently for the answer as to why these thoughts were suddenly invading my heart and soul. Considering my profession as a clergyman, did I harbor some guilt over the incredible past passion of which I shared with this woman so long ago?

Perhaps it was the stereotypical mid-life crisis, but it felt as if it was something very different, something much more than that, perhaps, it was some type of turning point for me in my life. I had mixed feelings over many things, my life, my career, and our children growing up so quickly it seemed as if life was becoming a blur. Honestly, I also had some concern about my marriage. I loved Binky with all my heart and soul, yet I wondered if I was a good husband and supported her as a husband should always support his wife, physically and most importantly, emotionally. Nagging thoughts of the present endlessly haunted me, but there were other thoughts of some concern. These thoughts were powerfully vivid and they were memories of my past. Something had seriously changed within me as of late; I had lost some energy, lost zeal, and my mind wandered from subject-to-subject with no clear focus. Perhaps I had reached a crossroads of some sort.

I just was not sure, but there was no doubt that it was weighing heavily upon me. My wife sensed it, she was too intuitive not to notice it, and she questioned me gently a few times, as to if I was feeling okay, but she mostly left it alone. Yet, I knew her too well, and she was watching me carefully, yet not invading my space unless it reached a precarious point in our relationship.

Perhaps, she felt this rather mundane, but a necessary task, would be a diversion for me for a few hours, or maybe, there was a whole lot more to her assigning me the cleanup chore than what it initially on the surface appeared to be.

A boring task, necessary or not, was not my idea of what I required right now in order to pull me out of this mood. Despite the firm warning, I still pondered the task for a mere second or two. You know, measure the risk, versus reward, of ticking off, dear Binky. No, mundane or not, it was not worth it.

"You got it, Binky. Done deal. Right now, I promise."

A few minutes later, I found myself sitting upon a stool, sorting through old cardboard boxes of accumulated stuff. I sorted it into a donation pile and a "chuck it away" pile. Old books, old hockey magazines, an old box of cigars that an old hockey coach gave me twenty years ago, and that I never smoked, and a baseball glove that was so old and cracked that it was crumbling. Honestly, none of this junk was any good.

I pushed aside box number one, pulled over a larger and much taller box, and opened it up. Immediately, a smile came over my face as I peered inside and saw that this box contained multitudes of my collections of fishing tackle and my old fishing pole. I reached for it, and in an instant, I held the pole in my hands.

It had been at least twenty years or even more since I

held this pole. It appeared to be in great condition. All the guides were still straight and tight, the enamel finish still glowed and I equipped it with that same familiar, high-quality open-faced spinning reel. Happily, and eagerly, I assembled the two sections of the pole together; I waved the pole in the air to duplicate a fishing cast, ran my fingers over the fishing line and studied the reel. There were so many wonderful and deep memories associated with this old fishing pole and reel. Many, many memories.

One or two of those memories, in light of my recent thoughts, sent a shiver down my spine when I recalled them. How strange to think of her and now to stumble upon my old fishing gear that had been tucked away for years and years.

This was all very strange indeed.

I wonder if my fly rod is buried somewhere deep inside that box? I will have to check. First, I wanted to examine my old spinning set up.

I held the pole in my hands and opened the bail of the spinning reel. I spun the handle of the reel and smiled when the bail snapped closed with a solid mechanical click. It still operated smooth as silk, even after all of these years. Sure, it might need a cleaning and a drop or two of oil, but there was no way that you could purchase a fishing reel of this quality any longer.

I waved the pole in the air again to simulate more casts. And that was it. I think I had an answer. A ticket out of the doldrums. Let me first finish this project, then return upstairs, and speak with Binky about an idea that I now have. Perhaps Binky had been praying for something to pick me back up too, and this assignment of hers had led me to this idea and a new ambition.

Fishing! Yes, indeed, it had been a long, long time since I wet a line or two.

Too long.

Where the River Bends and Curls

Chapter 1

The Old Pole

I stood in the icy cold stream, with my new hip waders on some ice cracking along the edges of the water, while I was tugging hard at the fishhook sewn to one of my prized nymphs. The other end of the hook was firmly stuck in the mouth of a small, but feisty, brook trout. A trout, which had taken my floating nymph as it tumbled down some curling rapids on a trout stream in Sussex County, New Jersey.

The fish had given me a bit of a tussle to bring in. Despite the size of the trout, the fish was strong and on a thin fly line leader; it was a challenging battle to bring the trout to my net. The hook worked free; I checked the trout for damage, and then gently placed the fish back in the water. I worked the trout back and forth in the water, until I saw the gills of the fish moving in and out, and his fins fanning in an effort to escape. I then loosened my grip. Off the trout sped, back into the rapids, and the fish was home again.

As I had learned a long time ago from a magical and captivating person who I fished with right here on this very stream, "The fun is in catching them, not in killing them!"

This section of the stream was not only a fly-fishing only stretch of the stream, but it was also a catch and release section. As long as the fish appeared unscathed by the hook, you had to return them to the water. It was fine by me to release the magnificent fish. Neither I, nor anyone else in our house, ate trout anyway! Downstream just a little farther, where the river bends and curls around some larger rocks and twists, I do recall a very special woman mentioning to me a very long time ago, is the location where the rules and regulations changed and they allowed you to switch over to bait-fishing. I wondered if that was still the case.

I stood there in the icy swirl of the waters for a few moments, enjoying the sunrise that was now peeking at me through some stark tree trunks and bare tree limbs. After the brief pause for admiration of God's magnificent creation, I reached in my pants pocket and took out my pocketknife. Quickly, I clipped the nymph off the end of the fly line and tucked the hook end of the little nymph into the rim of my hat. While folding the pocketknife up and placing it back in my pocket, I slowly and carefully made my way back to the banks of the stream.

I had been in the ice-cold water for well over two hours now, and despite my love of the cold, double thermal socks and heavy pants, I could feel a bit of numbness creeping into my toes. It was a good time to take a brief break. Two more trout caught today, and I reached my daily limit, anyway.

It was early April, and it had been a harsh winter in New Jersey. Generally, the first days of the opening of trout season usually bring some cold and somewhat wintery mornings, followed by spring-like afternoons.

With a current air temperature of about thirty-five degrees, this one certainly qualified as a wintry morning. Arriving on the edge of the stream, near to where I had established a small fishing camp, I found a good-sized rock, pulled my frozen legs out of the stream and pulled up the rock. It felt good to take some weight off my legs and to relax. I set my fly rod down on the stream bank, reached for my backpack sitting on the bank, and pulled out a thermos of coffee.

Oh boy, this was going to taste good!

I unscrewed the top to the thermos, poured a hot cup-o-Joe and sipped it.

Yes, indeed, it tasted good!

I sat there on the edge of a rock while, slowly sipping hot coffee, listening to the gentle ripple of the stream, and watching the sun decide whether it wanted to shine today or go back to sleep for a little while longer. The sun's apprehension was understandable, but we surely could use the warmth on this cold and early spring day.

I smiled, both inside and outside.

This little trout fishing excursion had contributed more to my soul than what I could have ever imagined, when I first ventured out a few days ago.

It was a spur-of-the-moment decision. All of this started with a simple cleanup mission a few Saturdays ago. While under strict orders from my dear wife to go through some old boxes, I pulled out from a basement closet, my old fishing gear, some tackle, my fishing vest, and before I knew it, dreams of a pastime that I enjoyed so long ago came flooding back into my mind. Mostly, even as old as the equipment was, it was surprisingly in excellent condition. I required a new pair of hip waders; the old ones rotted away from old age. However, the rest of the tackle, my spinning outfit and my fly rod were ready to go.

The cleanup details proved to be a turning point, because after I stumbled upon the old fishing gear, long since stowed away, I thought about how it had been forever and a few days more, since I had wet a line. It was time for some type of respite, and the discovery of the fishing tackle proved just the ticket that I required for some overdue rest and relaxation.

I had been working hard. Too hard. My dear wife reminded me of that fact too often and this was a sudden urge to relax, to catch my breath, and remind me of the beauty of God's creation.

What seemed as if it was just yesterday, but now, was many years ago, I received a promotion to the Office of Bishop of our Northeast Lutheran District. While I thought that I had prepared properly for the duties of being a Lutheran bishop, I must admit that I did not initially think that I was qualified for the job. Upon the assumption of the office, the duties caught me a bit on my heels. I had been thrilled in my position as the Senior Pastor of Reunion Lutheran Church. I had worked hard at the position for many years, and the church, which was on the brink of extinction when I first arrived, slowly climbed out of the ruins to become a vibrant and exciting place of worship. I was proud of our accomplishments at Reunion Lutheran Church, and I was somewhat taken by surprise and, to be honest, a bit reluctant to leave the church to serve as a bishop. Me? A long-haired hippie pastor who was now a bishop. Wow, it was all so overwhelming.

The duties were demanding, and the hours were long. Furthermore, I did not understand what I was doing wrong that caused the job to consume so much of my time.

My predecessor and former boss, who served as the bishop before me, and who was instrumental in my receiving this position, seemed to have tons of free time on his hands. In fact, it seemed as if all he did was play golf all day whenever the weather permitted him to do so.

Oh well, when I did some soul-searching and self-examination, I realized that I always tossed my heart and soul into all of my work and interests. My parents and my grandfather taught me that being a hard worker was a primary trait for success in life, and when you grow up lean and mean, in urban New Jersey, I do agree that it is important.

My trouble was in finding a balance.

Looking back over my life, be it in my former career as a

goaltender in professional ice hockey, or as an inexperienced pastor in a struggling church, to the position where I was right now in my life, I have always worked hard. In retrospect, perhaps too hard. I think it now was taking a toll on my life, my marriage, my family, my body and mind and, to a certain extent, my own well-being. It was time to admit that it exhausted me; I was now a victim of burnout. In addition, I was no longer a young man, nor was I a professional athlete who could practice hard all day and then play a perfect game that same night, and remain fresh and strong.

It all had caught up with me, and I needed to find a way to calm down, to relax, and to find that balance.

It was just that there was always so much to do. When I mentioned to my dear wife, Binky, that it had been forever since I had gone out fishing, she encouraged me to take a day off and return to the pastime to enjoy the relaxation. Her exhilaration at my change in direction was obvious and heartfelt. She sensed a new direction and attitude forming in her husband, and I think it inspired an outpouring of love and some emotion too.

We have been married for a long time now, and our love was still intense and very strong, but sometimes, as the years pass on, you mix your priorities into the wrong slots; you become complacent, relaxed, and you take your loved ones for granted. It might be time for me to wake up, smell the coffee, and for me to realize that they may not always be around. The last thing that I ever wanted to do was to alienate my wife or my family. No job, even serving God, is worth that to me, so perhaps it was now time for me to relax and reap some benefits of these many years of hard work. This brief fishing trip was my first step in that direction.

Our children were rapidly growing up, and they were now teenagers, enjoying the expansion of their own minds and interests. So perhaps it was time for their father to reexamine his priorities and commitments.

Those old hockey injuries were catching up with me now, the arthritis in my fingers early in the morning, painfully reminded me of those broken fingers caused by countless pucks smashing into them, as did the stiffness in my surgically repaired right knee and the soreness in other joints. I also noticed some wisps of gray hairs creeping into my long mop of what used to be reddish, blonde hair and a few more touches of gray in my facial hair too. I still wore my hair long, down past my shoulders. My wife would never allow me to cut it, but someday, I will be all gray and I will look like some kind of washed up, crazy hippie leftover from the 1970s.

Come to think of it, maybe that is what I looked like now.

After all, I was a Lutheran bishop.

Lately, introspective reflections of my past have captured my soul. I was now weary of it all, and for some reason, as of late; I had these strange nagging memories haunting me too, of a young woman, a woman, whom I lost along the way. I could not understand why I was thinking of her. It had been so long since she entered my mind. It was all combining to leave me very unsettled.

I prayed fervently for an awakening, a reexamination of sorts, and perhaps it was part of God's plan for me to arrive here at this trout stream on this fine morning.

Therefore, here I landed, on this cold, crisp morning, enjoying an amazing display of God's creation, sitting at this wonderful location, just above and near where the river bends and curls between rocks and twists. It was interesting, but this was a significant location in my life. A place I had visited before, a very long time ago, a special place in my heart.

Amazingly, here I was, after all of these years, back here again.

An inspiring location for a restart of sorts.

In the wild ride that we call life, this river and little jaunt of mine seemed as if it was a metaphor for a restart in my life. Often, our life is like a river, it bends and curls as it rolls along. Sometimes, the water runs high and hard, other times, it slows to a dreary trickle and barely moves, slightly stagnant and somewhat stale.

Here I sat on an uneven and sharp-edged rock, in between the bends and curls.

Now, I am so glad that I took Binky's advice, and I realized that this was very beneficial for my spirit. Fishing always provided me with some glorious adventures, with my boyhood friends, Jeff and Harry, and sometimes, without, but the memories were fond ones, and this trip was turning out to be a success. There was no doubt that it had rejuvenated my soul.

Another sip of coffee, a smile, and oh no, here come the ghosts! They float around me all the time, sometimes above my head, other times, all around me. The ghosts, oftentimes, encompass me, surround me and eventually, they capture my mind and soul. They are inescapable.

Between sips of coffee, I journeyed back in time. To a time and a place, when fishing for three young boys growing up lean and mean in a gritty New Jersey neighborhood, meant a trip to a dirty, chemical filled brook. Moreover, I recalled how our love of fishing, an old fishing pole, and fate, led me to a place in my heart and deep in my mind, to a place and to that same woman, of which I had been thinking about for quite a long time now.

A woman, whom I tried very hard to forget, but who had recently returned from within my deepest memories, and despite the passing of so many years, the memories of her haunted me once more. Those intense memories, along with other factors, were what I suspected were recently causing me such distress, such loss of focus, as my past had resurfaced. They were, in some ways, wonderful memories of a long, long time ago, yet they were excruciating memories of an unforgettable love affair, which I had with a certain, beautiful and very special, young lady.

"If you actually had a fishing pole, Paulie, then ya might catch a fish," my best friend, Harry M. Redmond Junior, pointed suspiciously at the stick that I held in my hand.

In actuality, I had cut down an old mop handle and proudly proclaimed it a fishing pole! By tying a fishing line on the end of the handle, I now was doing an extremely lousy job at pretending that it was a fishing pole. At least I now had an actual fishing hook on the end of the line. The bent safety pin that I was previously using for a hook did not make the cut. I shrugged my shoulders and frowned at Harry's comment. Right at this time, I did not have any extra money for a fishing pole. Christmas and my birthday were very far away, so this was the best that I could do for now.

The other member of our trio of our boyhood group, Jeff Porter, chimed in and commented, "Your pole sucks too, Harry. What is it like fifty years old or something like that?" Jeff pointed at Harry's fishing pole, which was indeed ancient. Harry had found it buried deep in his garage and his old man told him that the pole had been Mr. Redmond's older brother's pole. The pole did not have a working reel on it. The bail would no longer spin, so Harry had to use his free hand to peel the fishing line off and toss the line into the water.

"Yeah, yeah, yeah, well you suck too! You are the lucky one there, Jeffery. Ya pole is old, but it still works. At least you have a reel that spins."

Jeff looked at me, he smiled, and I guess he could not resist a comment. I did not blame him.

"It could be worse there Harry, ya could be Paulie and just have a mop handle!"

Jeff had an actual pole. It was his grandfather's fishing pole and was ancient, but it seemed as if it was in excellent condition. I still had no comment on my sad fishing situation, but vowed to scrape up some money and buy a real fishing pole soon. I had my eye on one that I had spotted in a thrift store, that was a few city blocks south of my home on Belmont Avenue. The store was obviously a front for illegal bookie and gambling activity, or even something worse than that, but I did not care. A few days ago, I spotted an old spinning outfit in the store window and I was certain that I could pick it up for a few dollars. Even at my young and ripe age, I knew that a fishing pole would not be in huge demand while on sale in a junk store on a main drag in Paterson, New Jersey!

Until then, I had no defense. After all, what is there to say, when you are holding an old mop handle in your hands?

There we were, three local boys, fishing in the local fishing hole.

Well, not exactly a fishing hole.

In the middle of this urban setting, tucked between old mills and factories that produced lace, twine and thread for the larger clothing and silk mills in nearby Paterson, New Jersey, meandered a small brook. A brook full of smelly chemicals, dyes, old hubcaps, wayward shopping carts, layers of colorful oil and gasoline floating on the surface of the water, and other assorted goodies. Amazingly, there were fish in the brook. They must have mutated and genetically modified themselves to be able to withstand the onslaught of weird chemicals, which poured into the water from a pipe poking out the side of the factory beside the brook.

The brook actually had a name, which I always felt was a strange and somewhat mysterious name. "Molly Ann's Brook" was the name of the brook, and I always wondered whom Molly Ann could have been or what she did to earn the honor of having a brook named after her.

In the mysterious and murky waters of Molly Ann's Brook, there lurked suckers, carp, a few catfish and the ever-present and most resilient of all fish, the sunfish, or as we called them, "Sunnies." Sunnies gave a new meaning to the word, "hardy." Sunnies could survive an atomic blast under the water. I swear they could. These genetically modified fish were so hardy; there was nothing that could kill them.

We could always count on catching a sunny or two. They would nip and bite at virtually anything shiny, or that remotely resembled bait of some sort.

The fish that swam around in the brook in front of us were the unlucky victims of high waters and snowmelt. They wandered down into the dubious brook, during high waters from a mysterious and mystical place found a few towns away. A place pictured in our young minds as a placid, pristine location, which we thought of as in the "country," miles upon miles away from our gritty city life. A place which we had only heard of existing here in the local folklore, a place known as Oldham Pond.

This wonderful and captivating place, held the key to how the poor fish ended up, in a twist of a sad and cruel fate to live out their lives in the chemically enhanced brook, rather than a placid and wild pond, full of clean, icy waters and jumping trout. Greater minds than ours told us that Oldham Pond would occasionally overflow a dam during rainy seasons, or floods, or during the late winter snowmelt. Since the pond was the source for Molly Ann's Brook that is where the fish washed over the dam, landed into the brook and eventually ended up on the end of our hooks, or sometimes, a bent safety pin or two!

There the three of us sat, on a dirt bank close to a bridge that passed over with the busy city street above us. Here, in this location, the brook ran deeper and slower and the chemical dyes cast an interesting array of fantastic colors while they floated on top of the slow-moving water.

Just up the brook, a few hundred feet or thereabouts, was the ultimate ugly fishing site. We called it "the square," because that is what it was. It was a concrete-walled square, located on the side of the brook, with walls that were about five feet high or thereabouts. The factory used the square as a source of constant water, a sort of pool to draw water from, and occasionally, when the waters of the brook ran high and over the top of the walls, fish would wash into the structure and remained trapped inside when the waters receded inside of the pool. Here, they suffered terribly in the deep stagnant waters of the square, constantly having to avoid the sucking action of the pipes drawing the water into the factory and then having to live in the chemicals pumped out of the discharge pipes.

Legend embroiled the square, ever since one of the locals from our gang and a schoolmate of ours, a young man known as "Big Wex" boasted to have caught a trout in the square after a heavy flooding period.

Yes! A real, actual trout!

The special fish, known as a trout, which to us existed in folklore and on the television, and fancy guys with fancy fly rods caught them in pristine streams high in the wild mountains of Colorado.

We only ever caught the same ugly types of fishes in the square, or something that could lightly fit the description of a fish. Nary a trout was in sight.

Most of the time, the foreman and the watchman from the factory would yell at us to get off the wall and, "Stay the hell out of the square!" He told us that we would be history if we ever fell in the water there.

Ah, the magic words to a ten-year-old boy. A challenge!

The brook, mostly, was a disgusting location to fish, but for three ten-year-old boys, growing up together in the rough and tumble world of urban New Jersey, it was all we knew.

If our parents caught us fishing here, then we would be in some serious trouble. They warned us constantly to stay away from the chemical-filled waters. I think they were afraid that we might grow another eyeball on our foreheads, but as you know when you are three mischievous boys, often, we consider our parent's rules as mere suggestions. Parenting was very different back then. You did not hang around the house playing video games, watching television, eating snacks and getting on your parent's nerves. You got your little ass kicked out of the house to go and entertain yourself and you had better stay out of trouble, too. Furthermore, you had better be home on time for dinner or chores, or you were really out of luck. Our parent's responsibility was to guide us, teach us, discipline us, feed and clothe us, but not to entertain us. You were on your own for that one. I swear that they would look in on me in my bedroom at the end of the day and see that I was alive and well, and figured they were good for another day.

Fishing in the brook was on the forbidden list, but so were many other things. We did it anyway and took our chances while figuring that we were relatively safe.

That is, until they caught us!

My old man, Harry's old man, as well as Mr. Porter, all had signed a reciprocal agreement that any one of them could beat our little asses silly whenever they caught us screwing up!

We caught a few fish that afternoon, but most importantly, we shared our friendship, a few laughs and some chemically induced whiffs of something we would most likely regret inhaling later on in our lives.

I vowed to return someday soon with a better pole. No, honestly, I vowed to return with an actual fishing pole, since my mop handle did not even loosely fit the classification of a fishing pole.

"Whadda ya want, kid? Guys like youse guys don't

need nuthin' we sell here in this store! I might be a lot of things, but I ain't sellin' them there girlie magazines on the shelf ovah dare to some punk ass kid. So don't even ask! Not yet, at least. Maybe in a year or two! But not now! Ya too young to see big, old, titties."

A short, grumpy guy with oily skin and slick-backed hair looked at me while he sat in the only chair in the entire store, behind a small glass display case and counter. He smoked a smelly stump of a cigar, and the smoke from the cigar encircled his head like some billowing campfire, only it did not smell quite as captivating. The remnants of the smoke dripped off the ceiling above the counter, like some disgusting and bizarre icicles of nicotine.

I looked over at him as my eyes scanned a few racks of well-worn merchandise that were for sale. In reality, it was all, mostly, a bunch of junk. Token items scattered about inside a store, in a rather poor and feeble effort to hide the true nature of the actual business conducted within this shady establishment.

Honestly, there was not too much legitimate stock for sale here, just a few sparse metal racks here and there, with some used clothing hanging upon metal hangers, a few worn-out wooden display racks sparsely filled with books, well-thumbed "girlie" magazines, an old toaster or two, and some kitchen items such as spoons, pans, knives and forks. There were some other assorted cardboard boxes of various sizes stacked in the corners of the store. One of the boxes had an old black and white television and a tube-type radio sitting upon them, but it was difficult to decide if they were for sale or just gathering dust.

Old Smelly was correct, because I should not be shopping or hanging around in this store. Yet, if there were a few attributes of which I possessed, they were that I was very street smart and I was brave too.

I also could run really, really fast.

All those factors were quite helpful to my survival in the

old neighborhood. I did not care about too much; right now, my eyes were on the prowl for the fishing pole.

"Ya need a good haircut, too. Ya look like ya a girlie girl with all that long hair!"

Old Smelly had a few choice words in referencing my long hair that always seemed to be a focal point of persons looking to get a few digs into me. I ignored him, and the smell of his rotgut cigar, now floating smoke through those same long locks of hair.

"So whadda ya want? If ya a smart ass, then I will toss ya out onto Belmont Avenue!"

I thought to myself how that would not happen. No way, with that big, old belly hanging over his belt, would he get a hold of me in order to do that! He moved way too slow.

"I saw a fishing pole in your window last week. I do not see it anymore. I was wondering, sir . . . if it was still for sale?"

"Sir . . . sir, sir! Ain't been no one who called me sir, in a long ass time kid. You are a long-haired girlie girl, but ya damn sure polite for a hippie kid. Yeah, yeah, yeah, I still got the pole. It is ten bucks with the reel included. It is umm . . . sorta of a collector's item. Ya might be polite, but you ain't got no ten bucks. So, why don't ya beat it, girlie girl?"

He stood up from the stool behind his "sales counter" and looked at me, took out a cloth from his pocket, and he wiped his brow of excessive facial oil while still smirking at me. Old Smelly took a long drag on the cigar and blew it straight up into the air. At least this time, he did not blow it directly towards me.

He was correct. Ten dollars was a ton of money. I only had two dollars to my name. I needed an action plan to raise funds quickly or I would be doomed to venture back out to the brook with my mop handle again. It was quite obvious the pole was not a collector's item. He wanted to get rid of me quickly, and if he, just by chance, successfully sucked ten bucks out of some stupid kid, then so be it.

I knew the drill.

"No, sir, you are correct. I do not have ten bucks. Thank you anyhow."

"Tough luck, kid. Ya, little hairy ass is shit outta luck. Ain't no good fishing around here, anyway. Just that chemical infested brook and ya should not be hanging around there, anyway. Ya might lose all that hair!"

That was an unusual variation on our parent's theme! I turned to leave the store and my eyes scanned the various layers of junk and "merchandise" in and around the dubious store. My eyes caught a little wooden box hanging out in a corner; a shoeshine kit, pushed aside and tucked away.

Immediately, I had an idea.

Good old-fashioned entrepreneurship. Even from a long distance, it was easy to determine that this was an ancient shoeshine kit.

Ah, hah! I found a method to earn a few measly dollars and creep closer to the angler's dream. I walked over to the box, knelt down in front of it, and opened the lid. Even without eyes behind my head, I could feel Old Smelly staring at me. I heard him puff his cigar and then sigh a little bit. His disappointment in me not leaving the store was readily apparent.

I was a resilient, fearless, and annoying kid.

Lifting the lid, my eyes skimmed the contents, and all the parts and pieces seemed as if they were in the kit. A few old cans of brown and black polish, a buffing brush, about four or five daubers to apply the polish, a few rags. The kit had all the supplies that you needed.

Now, I had never shined a shoe in my entire life, but I sat every Sunday night at the kitchen table and watched my old man shine and polish his black work shoes for the upcoming workweek. He would drag out his shoe shining supplies that he kept in an old cardboard shoebox in the cabinets underneath the kitchen sink. He would then sit in a chair and proceed to clean and polish up the work shoes. All the time, while he polished and buffed the work shoes, he would entertain me with the same story repeatedly. The old man would tell me how in the United States Army, if you could not see your face reflected in the toes of the dress shoes, then First Sergeant McIntyre would, "Kick ya sorry ass back to barracks to do them over again."

I can still see him there, in the kitchen of our family home at 182 Belmont Avenue, the distinctive odor of the polish floating in the air, the old man seated in a kitchen chair with his hand buried inside of the shoe. He would spit on the shoe, then rub the shoe furiously with the buffing brush and then another spit or two, and a few more rubs. . ..

I knew how to do it. I just needed to practice on some real shoes.

Here was a way to earn money.

I would see neighborhood guys a little older than I was, toting shoeshine kits such as this one, up and down the streets, slipping into the bars and gin mills and shining shoes for a few coins. It was a great business opportunity, after all, my allowance and newspaper delivery money had now dwindled down to mere pennies, and I needed another source of funding to supply my baseball and football trading card habit, buy a few new comic books, save for some hockey equipment and of course, fund my fishing interests.

Money was tight in our home, in fact, in our entire neighborhood; we all came from hard-working families full of tradesmen, truck drivers, mechanics, and general laborers. Your parents did not just fork up ten bucks on a whim. You received Christmas gifts, maybe a birthday gift or two, but in between, you earned what you needed.

There was no 123 Easy Street address stamped on the

mailbox on our home. Believe me, I checked and double-checked.

I thought this was a great idea. Yes! Shining shoes. All men wore black or brown shoes or boots! Furthermore, there was more than enough business to go around and share; there was a gin mill on every corner of our street and neighboring side streets.

Later on, in life, I learned that the small Borough of Haledon that I grew up in and the north side of Paterson had more gin mills, pubs, taverns and bars per square mile than any other location in America. That fact, for sure, explained an awful lot of the unusual behavior that I observed while growing up here.

I made my decision, stood up, and turned to see if Old Smelly was still watching me.

He was.

"Sir, how much will you charge me for this really, really, old shoe shine kit?"

I was a New Jersey kid and deal making was in my blood. I planted a strategically and very emphatically pronounced old description right away, hoping to lower the price.

Just for good measure, I decided to add an observation of the poor condition of the kit.

"One of the hinges on the back is broken and very loose. I might be able to fix it."

"Ah shit, kid . . . loose hinge, huh? Ya make it sound so friggin' serious. You, kid, are a major pain in the ass! How old are ya? You wheel and deal as if ya are an adult!"

"I am ten years old, sir. Almost eleven."

"Shit. Ya, almost eleven, huh? If it will get ya long-haired ass out of here right now, then give me a buck. I took two bucks off for the loose hinge."

I looked down at an old, faded price tag on the handle of the kit and screwed my face up a bit. The facts were the facts, and I was not afraid to point out the truth.

I pointed to the tag and said, "Sir, it says here, two dollars. You didn't take two bucks off."

"Shit, kid, whatever the hell it is! Ya want it or not? One friggin' dollar is the price!"

He blew a puff of smoke out and held out his hand. His patience had left him now, and I had successfully worn him down.

As I said, I was a resilient, fearless and annoying kid.

I briskly walked over to the counter, dug down deep in my dungaree pockets, and pulled out a one-dollar bill.

While I handed Old Smelly the dollar, two very shady looking guys emerged from behind a dirty curtain, which hung haphazardly across a makeshift doorway leading to the back of the store. I could only imagine what went on back there.

One of them looked at me, shook his head, and whispered to Old Smelly, "C'mon, get rid of the long-haired punk–ass kid. Jack is here, and he wants to place some dough down for this afternoon's ponies and buy some stuff to celebrate with too."

"Yeah, yeah, yeah, got it. Give me the buck kid and get lost. Get ya ass outta here now."

"Thanks! I will be back for the fishing pole. Say, if I gave you twenty-five cents, would ya hold it for me, sir?"

Old Smelly shook his head. He rolled his eyes and chuckled a little.

"Damn. Someday, kid, you will make something out of yaself, and escape this madness we call a city and shitty way of life. I can tell. This ain't no joint for a ten-year-old kid to be hanging around in. Ya are friggin' amazin' there kid! Ya ain't afraid of jackshit are ya? Ya got guts, kid. Ya got guts. More guts than some hotshot assholes around here do. You know the guys that I mean. Them assholes who are wandering around these streets actin' and makin' out they are tough guys. Give me a quarter and I will hold it for a week, kid. In the meantime, if you don't get the dough and I sell it, then you are shit outta luck and I keep ya quarter. Deal?"

"Deal! Here is the quarter."

I was now officially down to a few coins to my name and I was now the proud owner of a shoeshine kit with a very loose hinge.

While proudly toting my recycled shoeshine kit home, the few city blocks back to my house, I pondered my plan. I knew that a great deal of strategy was going to be required on my part in order to sell the new business idea of mine to my parents. The idea of their ten-year-old son wandering up and down the city streets, in and out of bars and corner gin mills, would not go over too well.

One obstacle at a time.

"Say, Dad, can I shine your shoes this time? I need the practice."

I decided the time was now right. Better now than whenever.

I held my shoeshine kit in my hands and stared at my father as he began his weekly ritual of preparing for the workweek. My father looked at me, then his eyes went down to the kit, which I held in my hand, and he squinted his eyes just a bit. The old man always did that with his eyes when he wanted to yell at me, but he decided he needed to gather more facts before he blasted me into orbit without a spaceship. I think he knew what I had planned without even asking. He shifted a little uneasily on the chair, and then he smiled a little.

Just a little.

"Where did ya get that shoeshine kit?"

"Bought it from the store down the street. You know . . . the junk store."

"The front for the bookie joint, the mob joint that I told you to stay out of, huh? Did Harry or Jeff go there wid ya?"

"Nah, I went in by myself. No need to call their fathers so that they get in trouble too. Yeah, I know what you told me, but he has this here, really cool fishing pole that I want to buy. I saw it in the window last week. I first need to earn ten dollars to buy it. The smelly guy in the store says the pole is a collector's item, and he wants ten bucks for it. He is a jerk and is ripping me off. It ain't no collector's item."

My father did not say a word. He just held his work shoes in his hand and slowly leaned back into his chair.

"Okay, Paulie, bonus point for honesty. I might hold off giving you a good, swift kick in the ass. So, how much did ya pay for the kit?"

"One buck and I put a quarter down on the pole to hold it."

"Let me guess, this smelly guy in the store told ya that if he sells the pole, before ya raise the dough, then you lose the quarter."

"Yeah, yeah, yeah," I said with a frown.

My father was a very smart man.

My dear Mum appeared from the dining room and she settled into a chair in the kitchen. She must have heard parts of our conversation, and now she, too, was interested in what her son had conjured up in his latest scheme.

My mother was English-born, the sweetest and the kindest woman that you will ever meet, but one should never interpret her kindness and sweetness as weakness. She protected her children, and her entire family, with the same ferocity that a Royal Navy battleship protects the English Crown.

Mum did not say a word. She slowly wiped her hands on a dishtowel that she hung from the waistline of her dress and listened, but initially, she did not say a word.

"So, Paulie, the plan is to shine shoes with this old kit, huh? Maybe go bar-to-bar, gin mill-to-gin mill, like ya have seen the older kids 'round here do? There is a kid, 'bout fifteen years old, who comes into the Widow's Pub when Gramps and I are having a few beers. He cleans and shines shoes up for a few bucks on a Saturday afternoon. This is your plan, huh?"

"Yeah, I saw the kit and thought that it might be a good idea. The guy in the store wanted more dough for it, but I showed him the hinge on the top was loose and he took a buck for it. It has all the stuff inside, but I might need new black polish. This one here is hard as a rock."

I bent down, set the kit on the floor in front of my father, opened the lid and my old man leaned over to study the contents, while I held up the hardened black polish. I snapped off the lid so that my father could see what I meant about the polish being too hard.

"How did ya fix the hinge?"

I pushed all my longhair away from my eyes, looked up at my father, smiled and said, "Wid a screw I found in your workshop. Fixed it myself."

I was proud of the repair and my deal making, too.

My father nodded, but still, he did not comment.

I sensed the pending doom looming on the horizon because of the lack of comments or granting of immediate permission from my parents. It was obvious they both admired my determination and ambition but did not agree with allowing me to run loose to practice my new trade in the world.

"Look, Paulie, the world is a rough place out there and gin mills ain't exactly where you need to be right now. There are lots of stuff that goes on in those places, well, geezzzz. You are a tough little kid, but. . .."

The old man finished his statement, but then he stopped and looked over at Mum. The old man was looking to Mum for help with this one. He did not want to blow up my dream without some guidance and support.

Mum smiled, looked at me, and sensed my pleading eyes.

"Paulie, I do hope this fishing pole is not for fishing in that horrible, Molly Ann's Brook," Mum stared intently at me, she knew better, but I stood there and shook my stupid head adamantly back and forth to suggest that was not the case. Mum took a deep breath, wiped her hands on the towel again, and sighed.

She knew that I was lying like a rug.

Mum forgave me for my fudging of the truth. She turned to the old man and said, "Paul, dear, you do go with Pop to the Widow's Pub on Saturday afternoon after work and enjoy a few beers. What if Paulie went with Pop and with you too? What if he promised that he would only go to the pubs with you or with Pop?"

I immediately, fervently, nodded to agree with Mum, while still avoiding a heartfelt confession on the actual fishing location. I then nodded even harder to show that I promised only to go with my grandfather (or as we always called him, "Gramps") or my father.

Mum always had my back. She smiled at my exuberance. I could tell that she, too, did not agree with or like my plan, but Mum did not want to discourage my ambition. Surprisingly, the old man answered rather quickly. It appeared as if Mum had the perfect solution.

Before answering, the old man screwed his mouth up a bit, and then he relaxed. He put his hand to his face, and he gently pushed his hair back across his forehead.

He softly agreed.

"Okay, yeah, yeah, yeah. I guess. Ya can only go with Gramps or with me. If I catch you doing otherwise, then that is the end of that shoeshine kit. I promise that I will kick ya ass from here to who knows where if I catch ya."

The old man studied my face; he waggled his finger towards me and nodded his head in agreement. After establishing the ground rules, he smiled and picked up the dauber from my kit.

"Here, take the shoe, ya right, this black polish is shot. Just shit can that old polish. Use mine. Tie all that long hair up, will ya! Ya can't see right with all that hair in ya eyes. Geez, how I wish ya would get a haircut."

He handed me the shoe, and I jumped at my chance to learn.

"Let me show you how we did it in the Army. That crab-ass Sarge McIntyre. Let me tell ya. He was one tough son-of-a-bitch."

That next Saturday afternoon, I was in the Widow's Pub, while gallantly wading my way through a maze of pipe and cigarette smoke. No one fainted and protested over the prospect of inhaling second-hand smoke back then. You inhaled more carcinogens when the city bus pulled away from a street corner than you did from inhaling a lifetime of exhaled cancer sticks. Either we are more educated these days or less fortified. I am not sure which is correct.

I was observing men sitting at the bar and at the well-worn wooden tables on the floor of the pub, for potential shines. In other words, I was scanning the crowd for shoes that were dull.

Suddenly, at such a young age, I was the epitome of an entrepreneur.

Most of the men were drinking beer and whiskey while intermittently cussing and laughing and occasionally glancing up at a nicotine-dulled television screen broadcasting a soccer match. In the smoky haze rising above the viewer's heads, an old television receiver was hanging bravely above the bar top. There I was on the floor of the pub, shining my first shoes and earning my first few nickels. I had to give the older kid who usually worked the pub a dime for moving in on his territory, but we worked a deal for him to work one side of the pub floor, while I worked the other. We also worked a deal by slicing the bar in half too.

I thought it was a fair deal.

The Widow's Pub was a local watering hole tucked on a street corner very close to our home. It catered to the large amount of English, Scottish, and Welsh population, which had settled into the neighborhood long ago to work in the

Paterson silk, lace, thread and cloth mills, which had emerged in droves, in what was now Paterson's legacy as, "America's Silk City."

When the big wars ravaged the mills and factories of England where they all worked, the English, Scottish, and Welsh tradesmen, who worked on the machines that produced the lace, silk and thread products, fled the United Kingdom and found work in America. More specifically, they gathered in and around Paterson, where the machines and trade were most familiar to them.

There now was a large population of families of a common heritage of the Queens' Royal Empire in our old neighborhood. I could never really imagine or fully appreciate, no matter how hard that I might try, what this group of people must have gone through in their lives. Seeing their homelands ravaged by the horrors of war, having to uproot their families, and in some cases, leave them, never to see them ever again in their lives. To journey off to a strange land, to start all over again, it is something that all of us must stop, pause, and think about occasionally. The horrors of what men can do to fellow men are oftentimes not fathomable. At least this little urban nook gave back to a special group of people, some of their pride, some of their honor, and a piece of their heritage to share once again.

My dad, well, he was a New Jersey and Paterson native, a street tough guy, who fell in love with an English gal. Gramps was Mum's father, and he was among the group who came across the pond and settled here in New Jersey while searching for work in order to keep his family afloat.

Gramps was the ultimate English tough guy, a man whose stories of toughness and prowess I could fill many pages of books and stories with, and slowly, someday, I vowed that I would. He had an accident in England as a young man and his left arm was now disabled, and because of many primitive operations, his arm never grew longer than the length of when the accident occurred, which was around my age or thereabouts.

As a result, as often is the case with a disability, other areas of the body compensate for the disabled parts. The blind person can hear a pin drop from a mile away, and the deaf person has the eyesight of a hawk. Gramp's right arm grew strong and powerful to compensate for the other arm's weakness.

Let me make one point very clear, that weak did not describe my grandfather in any way, nor in any manner. Either emotionally or physically, he was, without a shadow of any doubt, the toughest man that I ever knew, or ever would know!

The Widow's Pub was the most popular of the local watering holes in our neighborhood. It certainly was the most popular amongst the locals of United Kingdom heritage for tipping a few beers, watching a football (soccer) match on the tube broadcasting on a UHF channel out of Newark above the bar, sharing stories of the homeland and for gathering, much in the same manner, as they did back home.

"The Widow's Pub" was not the actual name of the pub. A chap from England, who died suddenly and tragically, had been the original proprietor of the establishment. Upon his unfortunate death, his wife took over the business, hence the new nickname. If I dug around really hard in my brain, someday, I might recall the actual name of the pub.

There I was, working hard, actually doing a good job at shining shoes.

One chap, after I completed a shine on his shoes, whispered to me that, "I needed a bit of a haircut, but I shined shoes better than the other lad did!"

The old man knew how to shine a mean shoe, and he had taught me well!

Gramps and my father sat at the bar, a few short feet away from where I worked on the floor of the pub, and they both kept a close eye on me.

They turned around often to check on my whereabouts, and Gramps at one point waved me over and instructed me to, "Shut your ears, Paulie boy. Do not repeat to your mum what you might see or hear in here. And don't let us catch you glancing at those girlie magazines sitting on the tables in the corners either." My father nodded his head, and I understood and agreed.

My father and Gramps always were very close, and they shared a few beers together, while all the men from across the pond poked fun at my father's hard New Jersey accent.

As tough as my grandfather was, my dad also was a bit on the rough side and he was not a man you needed to or wanted to tangle with! It was all in good fun. I quickly sensed that despite my father not being born in England, Scotland or Wales, he gained acceptance through my grandfather, and he was now one of the gang. As far as I was concerned, the locals quickly identified me as John Alcott's grandson, and that immediately put me within the inner circle.

I might have just as well have been born in Nottingham, England, the way they all warmly greeted and accepted me. A large part of that warm acceptance was because of the amount of respect my grandfather carried amongst his peers and fellow compatriots.

I was busy shining a chap's shoes when I suddenly heard some yelling and hollering. We all turned around to see an enormous man waving his arms in the air while shouting and spewing obscenities. The large man had been sitting on the first bar stool at the end of the bar closest to the front window of the pub. He now stood up and was quite angry.

The basis of his anger seemed to be something that the chap sitting next to him either said or did. It did not take too long to figure out that it was a dispute about the soccer (English Football) match on the television. The bartender quickly rushed over and tried to stem the tide of anger, but it proved to be fruitless.

The larger man pushed his comrade off the barstool, the smaller man went flying through the air, and he landed with a hard "thud" upon the pub floor.

"That'll teach ye to say that about Ipswich! Those bloody reds from the forest. They never will be half the team that Ipswich tis! I'll beat the bloody, bloomin' hell outta anyone whose is stupid 'nough to say different too!" The large man yelled in anger while he stood over the fallen and somewhat surprised man, who looked up at him from the floor.

I stood up, dropped my polishing rag, and looked over at my father and Gramps. Before I could react, and either Gramps or my father could say a word, the large man suddenly moved into action. He wobbled and could barely stand, and it was obvious that he was more than just a little half in the bag.

Stating his condition as simply being drunk was an understatement. Blitzed was the correct word to use in order to describe his condition. He could barely stand upright!

The chap whose shoes that I was polishing whispered to me as he put his hand upon my shoulder, "Oh, oh. He is a bit of a mean, old bastard, when he is ten sheets to the wind. Careful now, lad."

My heart raced. The other shoeshine kid ran out the front door in horror while I froze in my shoes. I watched as the large man went crazy, and he worked his way down the bar, taking each patron's beer mug or drink glass and tossing it over the bar and crashing them into the floor!

The barkeeper ducked the flying glass and alcohol baths and screamed for him to stop, "I'll call the police on you, Davison! I swear you'll go out in cuffs like you did a week or so ago! This time the widow won't drop the charges!"

Davison remained undaunted in his drunken mission.

He was an enormous man, one of the largest men that I had ever seen, and it appeared as if no one in the pub was willing to challenge or stop him on his drunken rampage.

I made a mental note, not to discuss English Football in any pubs now, or in the near future!

One-by-one, he went down the bar, grabbing patron's mugs and drinks and hurling them, and spewing drunken gibberish and angry poppycock in the air.

Gramps turned to me, waved and yelled as my father waved too, "Paulie boy! Over here, lad. Quickly! Stand in here between your father and me!"

I quickly gathered up my shoe polishing equipment, ran over to the bar, followed my grandfather and father's direction, and tucked between them. I stood there as Gramps put his hand on my shoulder and my father did not move, but he just calmly sipped his beer and stared ahead. Gramps sat on a bar stool closest to where Davison was working off his drunken rage, and when Davison finally reached over and tossed aside the drink of the man who was sitting close to us, he made the fateful mistake of reaching for my grandfather's beer mug.

Quick as a flash, Gramps reached out with his good arm, and I saw the muscles in his arms ripple and bulge. As long as I will ever live, I will never forget the pain on Davison's face as the power of the grip of my grandfather's hand on his arm caused the immense man's knees to bend and buckle in sheer agony.

The giant man was helpless.

"Davison, you bloody, drunken, bloke," Gramps said while tightening his grip, "if you touch my beer or my son-in-law's beer, or even brush or just barely tap into the young lad here, I will break ya ass into ten pieces. I then will toss what I leave of your ass through the front glass of the pub and they will have ta' ship your bloomin' ass, or what I might leave of you, back to Ipswich in a bloody pine box."

Davison looked at Gramps through shipwrecked eyes and even in his intense pain, he nodded in acknowledgement of the warning that Gramps gave him.

Gramps let go of his arm, Davison staggered backwards, leaned in and said, "Sorry 'bout that John, old chap. I am a bit on the wobbly side here. Certainly, there was no ill offense meant. I do regret causing a ruckus around you and your time here at the pub. Furthermore, I assure you that I do understand about the pine box. Your reputation precedes you, old boy."

I stood in amazement watching while my father and Gramps went back to calmly drinking their beers. Davison went around Gramps, he went around my father, and continued with his drunken glass and mug hurling with the poor chap seated next to my father.

As the aftermath of the wild incident settled in and I heard the wailing of police sirens echoing out in the city streets, Gramps turned to me and said, "Now, Paulie boy, keep this one to just us. No need to tell your mum. Understand?"

I pushed all the long hair out of my eyes and nodded my head emphatically to signal my agreement. My father studied my face carefully for any residual fear or apprehension over the turmoil.

There was no fear.

I was a fearless kid. As Old Smelly in the front for a bookie joint had correctly labeled me, there was no doubt that I was not afraid of jackshit. Later on, in my life, I would not only prove that fact but also, I would come to realize that it would serve me well. No doubt, it came from my gene pool.

My father seemed satisfied at my reaction and he smiled at me, as did Gramps.

My grandfather put his hand on my shoulder and he softly said, while gripping my shoulder tighter, "A lesson for you, Paulie boy. This afternoon was a lesson for you.

Always stand up for what is right and true, never back down when you need to protect your own, and always be true to your honor. If you believe in your heart, in what you have done, and you did the best you could, then I assure you that you will have no regrets. That is my advice for you, Paulie boy. Never have regrets about what you have done. Regrets are for fools. Regrets are only foolish doubts of decisions that we have made. They serve no purpose. They only cause us angst and worry. Make a choice, be a man, then move on. Never doubt."

Considering his abhorrent behavior and in his meager and somewhat shallow defense, Davison did not complain too much when the police officers slapped the handcuffs on him and the officers carried him out to the squad car. In retrospect, it might have been a better fate than if he had decided not to listen to the warning that my grandfather had given to him.

I learned a powerful lesson or two that afternoon in the Widow's Pub. Not the least of, was that you work hard, earn what you work hard for, even if it means shining some shoes for some random bloke in a gin mill. I came away from that fateful afternoon with more money than I had ever earned in one day in my short lifespan. In addition, believe me; I earned every measly penny too! I also learned that you always stand for what you believe in. Backing down from what is right or true was not part of my spirit. Looking back, I realized that when Davison told Gramps that he regretted his actions, he was a fool. He was the man who became three sheets to the wind. He acted as he did, and was in control of his own actions. His regrets, although on the surface were valid, labeled him as a fool. He should never have allowed himself to be in that position to begin with! The lessons that Gramps and my old man were trying to teach me became clearer. If you make a decision, then stick with it, stand up for it, admit it and move on.

I was very lucky to have such philosophical wisdom teaching me at such a young age. Life's lessons come at you hard, but they stay with you forever.

"Man, that is one ugly ass catfish ya caught there, Paulie," Harry observed as Jeff leaned over Harry's shoulder to watch me reel the catfish into the dirt bank.

I set the fish down on the bank, put my boot on the fish and worked the hook out of his mouth. Catfish always make a funny, squishing noise whenever you would squeeze them and those barbs hurt if you try to hold them in your hands. We learned that the best way to pull the hook out was with them lodged underfoot.

A gentle kick with my boot and the fish fell back in the chemically enhanced water.

"Nah, it was not too bad looking," I said.

In my mind, it was the perfect fish, ugly or not. It was the first fish that I had ever landed, with my new fishing pole that I forked up (much to the surprise of Old Smelly) nine dollars and seventy-five cents for a day or two earlier.

After all, the pole was a collector's item. In addition, there is something very special about earning something on your own, with hard work, wheeling and dealing with shady foes and an earnest commitment towards a goal. I also knew now, to stay away from English football discussions in pubs, and that your reputation and your honor are sometimes worth more than you can ever realize.

Yes, indeed, I had learned a powerful lesson or two, or perhaps I had learned even a bit more than I could ever realize.

Chapter 2

Sparkling Eyes

Jeff, Harry, and I spent many days fishing together. When we grew older, we eventually branched out, and left that horrible chemical infested brook behind. We pedaled our bicycles far into the outskirts of our usual roaming, and found the coveted source of Molly Ann's Brook, a body of water called the Oldham Pond. The pond was not quite as pristine in our minds as we had imagined that it would be. No, much to our dismay, it did not have sparkling waters, with pristine, tumbling, spring-fed waterfalls feeding the pond; yet it was, in our minds, quite beautiful.

The pond was actually located only about five or so miles from our old neighborhood, and the setting was surprisingly idyllic.

If you closed your eyes on the journey, and appeared on the shores of the Oldham Pond, you could easily imagine that you might have traveled to a lovely location in Vermont or New Hampshire. Urban New Jersey and all of its hard-core grit, indeed, has several carefully concealed hidden gems within its hard-boiled confines.

The Oldham Pond was on the edges of the Borough of North Haledon. The pond was found, in what was actually a surprisingly, glorious backdrop of scenic beauty, along the side of a main road that led all the way to the very center of downtown Paterson, New Jersey, to the towering background of High Mountain, which loomed above the pond in the distance.

Certainly, it was very different in settings and appearance from the poor, lowly, chemically enhanced Molly Ann's Brook.

Furthermore, at Oldham Pond was where we caught our first trout and where we had to possess actual fishing licenses. On one very fruitful opening day of trout season, when I was lucky enough to catch my State of New Jersey mandated limit of trout at the pond, I managed to have my picture taken and plastered into the Paterson Evening News newspaper in the sports and the outdoor section! I felt as if I was world famous. . ..

Between our favorite pastimes, which were playing hockey, on the street, on roller-skates and then on the ice, I would say that fishing was next in line. It provided us with an outlet in the great outdoors and a quiet camaraderie.

Collecting nightcrawlers for bait, which are the big, giant worms that come up for air and lay on fertile soil in the springtime of the year, or after heavy rains, became a hobby in itself.

We had one adventure, where we cut through some private property in our quest for worm collection and ran into an immense German Shepherd dog named Sweetheart, who did not take too fondly to our encroachment on her territory. She chased us for a few backyards. Harry climbed up into a tree, Jeff hid in some shrubs, and as verification to the fact that I was a quick runner; I ended up in the next county.

Lucky for us, Sweetheart really *was* a sweetheart, and she wanted to lick us more than tear us apart.

In what I always felt that was a tribute to our upbringing together, the strong friendship in which the three of us shared, both during fishing, playing hockey or other activities, is the one thing that we can now recall, more than any other aspect of our adventures together.

The three of us would sit together on the edges of the Oldham Pond, talking about every subject imaginable from young women, to cars and trucks, of course hockey, and fishing too.

We also had a secret fishing weapon, discovered quite by accident.

If no fish were biting, nor any fish caught, or were even nibbling on our endless selections of worms, nightcrawlers, bugs, live minnows and lures . . . then Jeff would pull out his trusty harmonica.

Jeff kept a harmonica in his pocket, and Jeff, as well as Harry, were talented musicians. I could strum four cords on a six or twelve-string guitar, and that was about it. My broken fingers, because of playing the position of goaltender in hockey, did not allow the flexibility required for properly working a fret-board.

Yet, when things were slow in the fishing world, all we had to do was look over to Jeff and he would nod his head, pull the harmonica out of his pocket and begin to play. He could play all kinds of tunes, but the tune that he played most often seemed to be the melody of some sad, old, love song, of which I don't even know or recall the name.

A few notes and BANG! A hit or two on the lines! Then a fish or two was happily reeled to shore.

It was our secret weapon.

I still fished with and used my old trusty fishing pole, or as I occasionally still called it, my collector's item. It proved to be a wonderful pole; the reel was smooth, strong and steadfastly reliable. The ten dollars, which I spent on it, proved to be one of the best investments of joy versus money spent in which I had ever made.

Yet, as the three of us fished together throughout all of our boyhood years, and into the cusp of adulthood, I fished with not only Jeff and Harry. Jeff eventually went on his own way, following a beautiful young woman whom he would eventually marry. Harry and I continued our way.

We fished together occasionally, in fact, one time, and we even bought a rickety old boat together for what turned out to be an ill-fated adventure.

However, it turns out that the most powerful fishing experience that I would have arrived from an entirely different direction. It turns out that my introduction to using something other than my old, trusty spinning reel and pole when I fished, and receiving a lesson in wetting a line with a fly rod while fly-fishing for trout, actually came from a rather different and surprising teacher. . ..

My goodness, what a teacher she was, too!

She was the source of my nagging memories, the thoughts that all were deeply set within my mind. The steely reminders of my past that, as of late, I could not shape, bend or break. We shared some special times together, wonderful times, during what I do believe that was a once in a lifetime meeting, perhaps a once in a lifetime love. I will never forget her, or what now are some dusty, old memories.

Renee Gorman was short, petite, and beautiful. At first glance, you would say that she was cute. After a close and more careful observation, she was beyond cute, and you would step back and say, "Oh my, that is some gorgeous young woman there."

No doubt she was indeed beautiful.

She had jet-black hair, which she cut very short, she wore dangling but small, teardrop-shaped, white gold earrings in her earlobes. I never saw her wear any more or any less than those earrings in her ears.

Well, come to think of it, that is not true. There was one time when I saw her not wearing them. . ..

The earrings were a perfect selection; they complemented her face well; they were as diminutive and petite as she was. Funny, how when you recall certain features of a person, specific things stick in your mind, small things, such as the type of earrings that Renee wore.

Well, other things stuck in my mind too!

Renee generally always wore long skirts or dresses. They all were tight at her waist, and they enhanced her shapely figure. The dresses and skirts tended to be longer than the more commonly worn casual styles, which were popular in women's fashion at the time. Her skirts and dresses flowed wide as they left her waist and gently flowed around her ankles in an alluring manner. Most of the time, she wore solid colors, both in her skirt and dress selections and in her choice of blouses. Dark blues, black, dark red, all varieties of dark colors, which only enhanced her appeal and locked step with the fact that Renee Gorman had her own sense of style, she was going to be her own woman, and it was unique and full of allure. Renee always wore low-heeled, elegant shoes, and never tried to add to her height. She was comfortable in her own skin, and it was for an excellent reason. She was an astounding woman.

She possessed a dazzling smile, with perfect, white, shining teeth. Amazingly, not a single tooth in her perfect mouth was out of alignment or bent in any manner.

Perfect teeth and a perfect smile.

When you are a professional ice hockey goaltender and you are usually nursing some type of chopper malady of your own, and you surround yourself with fellow hockey players who most likely were nursing the same issues, you had a tendency to admire a perfect set of teeth!

She came from a well-to-do, upper-middle class family. They all lived in a majestic, upscale house in a quiet suburb of Paterson. Renee's mother and father both had important jobs, which obviously paid handsome incomes and provided solid employment.

Renee once told me that her parents had spent a lot of

money on her teeth.

She had a striking figure, with perfect breasts, a very slim stomach and waistline, yet her hips and the rest of her curves were generous in all the correct locations! No doubt, she was gorgeous. She was female perfection personified.

Early on in our brief relationship, we went on a double date with Harry and his longtime girlfriend, Joyce Dilber. The next day, after our date, Harry went on and on about how I needed to shed the "Mr. Nice Guy" approach, as well as the dreaded, "Old Lady Syndrome" he claimed that I was afflicted with these days. He thought Renee was as fine as fine could be, and I do think he had a valid point.

Harry, in his bombastic and often crude descriptions of young women, described Renee's best asset as "Being behind her now," and while that might certainly be correct and accurate, to me, her eyes told me her true story.

Ah yes, her figure, hair, appearance and smile could captivate you. But then there were those sparkling brown eyes. Her eyes sparkled as if they were illuminated glass. They were glowing and dark brown in the centers, and then gradually they became opaque and lighter along the edges.

Watching a person's eyes all the time became a habit of mine during my hockey career, where the eyes of the shooter could provide you with the secret to where the puck was going to end up. I adapted the habit into the "civilian" world and as a pastor; it actually helped me in more ways than I ever imagined from when I first developed the habit. I could study a congregation's eyes collectively and individually from the pulpit, and decide if my sermon or words were boring the stuffing out of them, or if I had a hit upon a nerve. I always focused upon the eyes of a person, it led me to see so much more of them and sometimes, I could see into their soul. It also helped me greatly in counseling sessions, and when to know that my dear wife was not too happy with me!

Renee Gorman was a stunning young woman, equipped with a harsh tongue, a kind, but sharp and an often-snarky personality. She also possessed a great deal of wit and intelligence and then above all, Renee Gorman's eyes were something of which I would find very hard to forget.

She was unforgettable.

The two of us had a rather awkward start to our relationship. . ..

"Can I help you? It looks as if you are having a bit of car trouble, eh?" I asked a stunningly beautiful woman standing next to the car that was currently parked next to my jeep. I had walked out of Ice Land Arena after a hockey game; a game where our team, the Long Island Roosters, had lost a hard-fought battle, by the score of two to one. I allowed the game winning goal under rather dubious circumstances, a rolling and bouncing puck that I usually stop, but in this case, it was not my best performance.

Oh well, maybe, in my heart, I now sought a bit of redemption by assisting the gorgeous young woman with her car troubles.

"Eh? Eh? Hmm. . .. Okay, now! Unusual language. Ah, yes. I can see that you have long hair, way past your shoulders, all kinds of facial hair, but you can still see okay, all that hair is not in your eyes. Therefore, you have proven that while you might be a dumb ass, you certainly are not a blind, dumb ass. The equipment bag, which you are carrying, tells me that you must have played in the boring-ass hockey game, that my now former boyfriend forced my gorgeous ass to watch. I have to say that you must be a friggin' damn genius to determine that I have car trouble."

She folded her arms across her ample breasts and I admired how her shapely figure bulged a bit out of the top of her low-cut blouse.

Well, after all, a man could not help but notice.

She then continued to blast me, "Let's see now. We can take a little more time to analyze this situation. Ah, huh, my car's hood is up and I am standing in the middle of this horrible parking lot next to this wretched, friggin' car that will never start when I need it to!"

I did not know how to answer her, but her aloof attitude at a time of need did in fact have some type of strange appeal. Although her vehicle was malfunctioning, there was little doubt that this woman could take care of herself. My goodness, she was short in stature, but I could tell that she was quite opinionated and more than just a little rough and tumble, and her language, well, it was well suited for the hockey rink.

In addition, she surely was easy to look at!

Undaunted, I chuckled a bit at her overwhelming reaction to a simple and rather innocent offer to help her. I set my equipment bag down next to the jeep, reached into the back pocket of my dungarees, and pulled out a hair tie. I pulled all of my long hair back and tied it off with the tie, and then I smiled at her.

"Wait! Shit," she pointed at me and said, "damn! All that hair, I recognize you now. Believe me, every woman in the stands at that stupid ass hockey game tonight knows who you are too! You are the goalie for the team from Long Island. Oh, wow! My now, ex-boyfriend dislikes you, but his stupid ass, reluctantly admitted that you are the best goalie in the league."

She waved her hands at me while she spoke, but now her posture relaxed and her face changed a bit. It seemed as if she sympathized with me just a little and her previously harsh posture softened as she actually walked a few steps closer to the side of my jeep.

The young woman commented, "You lost the game. Sorry. I know shit about hockey and in fact, I hate it because he loves it, but I have to say that even I can tell that you are very good at what you do. By the way, the winning goal was not your fault. I think your own player was a stupid shit, and he knocked it in the net by accident."

She returned my smile and melted my heart a bit. Oh yes, she had softened up considerably.

"Maybe. I usually stop those types of shots, but tonight was not my night. Thank you for the compliment, you are very kind."

Now, it was my chance to walk a few steps closer and see where this conversation would lead me, "Let me pause here and put my genius cap on and determine that this hockey loving, now ex-boyfriend and you, had a bit of a spat and he has now taken off on you. You took separate cars to the game, planned to go out for dinner and perhaps a few drinks afterwards, and after your argument or perhaps a bitter disagreement of sorts, you find that your car will not start and you are now stuck here, next to some long-haired hippie, ice hockey goalie's jeep."

I had to admit that I was turning on a bit of charm, because when I finished with my assessment of the situation, I folded my arms across my chest, and on purpose, in order to gauge her reaction, I flexed some of my arm muscles and smiled at her.

I then asked, "So . . . how did I do, eh?"

She leaned back on the car, her eyes sparkling in the light from the parking lot pole light above our heads; she too folded her arms across her chest and smiled at me.

"You might not appear to be very smart, you know, by standing there in front of that net thing while wild, hulking assholes throw rubber pucks at you. All the time, while you wear some stupid looking leather suit of armor, but you know what they say about books and covers and such."

"I have heard that a time or two. Yes, indeed. Say, as a struggling goalie, facing hulking bruisers who try to kill me most every night, while earning a whopping sum of seventeen dollars per game, I know about unreliable vehicles. I carry tools with me all the time because, well, my jeep is old, and at times, it gives me fits. My old man taught me to carry tools in my vehicle, our family cars generally were piles of junk, and he taught me how to repair them too. If you would like, I can grab the toolbox and see what I can do for your car. Oh, and by the way, no offense taken."

She laughed aloud, waved her arms and hands at me, smiled widely and said, "None given! You are a rough, tough, goalie. I am sure you can handle a little verbal abuse from a cute little woman such as I am. Eh?" She poked fun at my mixed-breed English and New Jersey accent.

I reached out my hand and introduced myself, "Hi. I am Paul John Henson. Most everyone just calls me number twenty-seven, or Paulie."

She took my hand and grasped it gently. Her touch was soft and smooth and her tiny hands eclipsed inside of my giant paws.

"Renee Gorman. Nice to meet you, mistah goalie guy. I apologize for the piss-poor attitude and verbal onslaught. It just has been a horrible night."

"Apology accepted. I can imagine. Disputes and fights with loved ones are always. . .."

Renee cut me off by screaming, "EX LOVED ONE! I SHOULD HAVE DUMPED HIS SORRY FAT ASS A LONG TIME AGO!"

I playfully ducked and threw my arms up over my body in jest, as if to deflect her anger while her words echoed over my head and across the parking lot.

She laughed again, and said, "I must say, you have such a wonderful dry sense of humor. And, shit, you sure are a lot larger in person than you look when you are on the ice. My goodness, you are tall and muscular. Maybe six feet five, or thereabouts? I am short as short can be, and I feel as if, right now, that I am standing next to a damn tree."

"Yeah, yeah, yeah, I am around that height. I guess. It has been a long time since a hockey club measured me for my height. Everyone tells me that I am larger in person than I look when I am in goal. I think that I must hunch over a lot."

"Damn straight, more friggin' handsome too. I thought you looked good from far away. It was hard to tell with all that stupid shit that you wear while playing that ridiculous game. Nevertheless, when you pulled the goalie mask off at the end of the game, I thought that you looked hot. I have to say that so did the woman sitting next to me, who told me she had seen you at a game once before. I will not repeat her words, even if I thought about them on my own, because she was a little lewder in her comments towards you than I am willing to be right now. Oh sorry, if I am drooling over you a bit. I tend to be outward and honest, and I call it as I see it, but damn, mistah goalie guy, you can take a lady's breath away."

We locked eyes on her comment and if not for the wretched affliction of the Old Lady Syndrome, I would have commented on her beauty; however, Renee recovered before I could even make a comment, even if I could have. I cannot say that she suffered from some embarrassment from speaking her comments about my appearance because as I would come to know and understand Renee Gorman better; I doubt that anything could ever embarrass her. It was more as if she was sputtering a little over a heartfelt reaction, almost as if she had said the words spontaneously, without thinking about them.

Despite her slight stall, she recovered quickly. Her eyes looked away from mine; she then walked over to the front of the car and stared down in the engine while waving her hands expressively over the source of the lack of her forward propulsion abilities.

She looked back at me and said, "Sure, sure, sure, please, if you can resurrect this damn car, I would be forever indebted to you, the sort of the damsel in distress type of bullshit."

"I will see what I can do. No promises, though . . . and no charge. If I get it rolling, then you do not owe me anything."

I grabbed my toolbox from the rear compartment of the jeep. I had to admit that my heart was pounding a bit here. Her eyes, her beauty, her comments, her language and her toughness—she was quite the young lady.

I think that I was a bit smitten.

"Try it now, Renee. Crank it slowly."

A turn of the key, a sputter or two, and BANG! The engine turned over, and it was soon running smoothly. In reality, it was a very nice car, just lacking a bit of maintenance.

"The battery cables were all loose. I did the best I could, but you need new ones. The cable terminals were all loose too, as well as the wire cables. I am afraid that if they work loose again, the car's engine could die at any time. You need the battery to start the engine as well as allow it to store a charge and keep the engine running too."

"Shit, geeky-ass, long-winded explanation. I would not think you were so damn in-depth with mechanical shit. Anyway, thank you, goalie guy. I do owe you."

"Nah, nah, nah, you do not owe me. Say, if you would like, I will follow you home. If the cables come loose, the engine will not run long and you will be stuck on the side of the road. Do you have to go far?"

Her voice softened greatly, and she smiled widely, while speaking in a low, almost husky tone. Parts of my body twitched in response. My goodness, this was a special woman.

Her eyes sparkled even more while Renee said, "Why no, I live only a mile or so away from here. You are very kind. I feel bad now, for how I previously spoke to you."

"Don't feel that way. I am a rough, tough, goalie guy 'member? Let's roll before it dies again, eh?"

She nodded, jumped in the car, closed the door, yelled for me to follow her and I packed the tools up, threw my equipment bag in the jeep, and climbed in my old bucket of bolts.

I followed her down the main drag for a mile or so, then we made a few turns off the main road. She drove fast and aggressively, effortlessly, zipping in and out of the traffic. I down-shifted and then I shifted the gearbox up into the highest gear on the old jeep in an effort to keep up with her. Her aggressive driving certainly fit her personality! I could only imagine some of the words she was using to describe the drivers who were not keeping pace with Renee Gorman! We worked our way off the main drag, and then we sped through some upscale, commuter type neighborhoods.

She did indeed; live very close to the Ice Land Arena, only a mile or so away. We pulled into a long street, a street with a slight incline, in an upscale subdivision of lovely split-level and tri-level homes, with fine-trimmed lawns and carefully maintained streets.

Very different from my old neighborhood.

I pulled the jeep along the curb in the front of her house and watched as she parked the car in the driveway, in front of a three-car garage. I studied her while I watched as she shut the engine off, opened the door, and she sauntered to the jeep. She came over to the driver's side of the jeep. I left the engine running. I think that I purposely did so as if to show that I had no ill intentions or wild expectations.

"Thank you once again, mistah goalie guy. Seriously, you are very kind."

I nodded and said, "You are very welcome. It was my pleasure. Hey, please make sure that you replace those cables and terminals very soon. There is not always a long-haired, hippie, ice hockey goalie with tools and junky jeeps, hanging around in parking lots. Not one, at least, who can talk and perform geeky-shit."

"I like your style, mistah goalie guy. Please, I am not being rude, and I guess that I am being slightly forward towards you, but I have to say that I would invite you inside for a cup of tea or coffee, but I live with my parents."

Renee looked away from me and I caught her eyes looking up and over the top of the jeep towards the house as if she was checking to see if someone inside the house was watching us.

She then explained, "I guess you could tell that already by the type of house and neighborhood, it is not exactly the kind of residence for a single girl to be livin' in. I am a struggling college student trying to live off campus until I get my head on tight enough to decide what I want to do with my life."

"Nothing wrong with that."

"No, there is not, but as you may have noticed, I am a slightly forward person, who generally speaks her mind."

I feigned some phony shock and awe and grasped my chest, while saying loudly, "No! Renee, I did not notice!"

She laughed loudly, gently grabbed my arm, and our eyes locked once again.

She almost whispered to me now, while she leaned in close and said, "I am Jewish. I mean, not just the run of the mill, Jewish. We are quite strict in my house as far as our religious beliefs are concerned. We are really, really, Jewish. I can tell that you are not. Perhaps I am incorrect, but I doubt it. By some wild chance in Hell . . . are you?"

I gently shook my head and smiled, "No, Renee, I am Lutheran."

"Oh shit! That would go over like a friggin' atomic bomb exploding in my living room. We had some relatives that did not fare so well over there."

"Your parents are practicing and very strict, eh?"

"Yes, and for now, even though I am my own woman, you know, living under their roof, their rules, you know the drill. One look at you, those blonde and red locks of hair hanging down all over Anglo-Saxon features, light skin, then you would speak with that weird accent. One, 'eh out of your mouth and well. . .. You, despite my previous rude comments, seem remarkably intelligent, so I guess that you understand."

"I do, and I respect all religions and all rules. I think it is exceptional that you are cognizant and respectful of your parent's wishes. That is awesome, Renee, it really is. Plus, the long hair, the beard, the hippie look, the rock-and-roll tee shirt, canvas sneakers, the ice hockey goalie, a poor guy from the old city neighborhood, right? I imagine that I have a number of things stacked against me, eh?"

Renee nodded, reached inside the window of my jeep, and motioned for my hand. I reached over and she gently took my hand in hers. After she squeezed my hand tightly, Renee gently pried my hand open, tugging on one finger at a time. She placed a piece of notepaper in my hand, and then very slowly and seductively folded my fingers over it. She smiled again and melted my heart, with those incredible eyes wildly sparkling in the now, almost pitch black, darkness.

"Respectful, yes, fully adherent, well, no. I don't even wear my headscarf according to the rules. Only when I want to wear it. I break Jewish rules all the time. Right and left. I am my own woman, goalie guy. Please, damn, please call me, as I said, you can take a lady's breath away."

Of course, the next day, I told Harry about the fabulous woman whom I met by chance in the parking lot of the arena. He in turn told his on again and off again, and sometimes steady girlfriend, Joyce Dilber, about her too, as well as the entire Redmond family! Harry ranted and raved about my various afflictions, Joyce, as well as Harry, and Harry's family all coached me, and they told me what a fool that I was for not calling her the next day!

Harry was very often correct about my behavior, and I instantly mustered up a million excuses, "Renee is Jewish. I am Lutheran. Her family is wealthy. I am dirt poor. Her parents would not approve of me. I am working late today. I have hockey practice tomorrow. It is the end of the season. . ..”

Millions of them. Excuses, excuses, excuses, and all of them were lame and not valid. However, the truth was that her enchanting eyes followed me in my dreams most everywhere I went.

Day and night.

About one week later, upon continued prodding from both Harry and Joyce, I finally mustered up enough courage to call her, hoping and praying the entire time that Renee answered the telephone, and not her parents. She did.

As of late, I had not had too many girlfriends. This was at least two years before I met my eventual wife, Binky Hobnobber, and the primary focus of my mind was upon a career in professional hockey.

It was that same old obsession for Paul John Henson. Hockey was my life, my career, and a passion. It had invaded my soul, heart, and mind, and there was very little room left for any young women.

At one time, I did have one woman. She was a special gal, a certain young woman named Maureen Zipperelli. Maureen was my sister’s best friend. We all grew up together, and she was a little older than I was, but as we grew up together, we also fell in love together.

I did not know it at the time, or I knew it and I was too stupid or too afraid of admitting it, but I had fallen in love with her. However, as usual, hockey was in the way.

Harry often lectured me that I was being a complete fool regarding my relationship with Maureen. He could never understand why I had such cold feet, but Harry did not feel what I felt inside of my heart. I knew I could easily fall head over heels in love with Maureen, and hockey, and my dreams would slip away forever.

On the other hand, maybe Harry already knew the truth, and the truth was that I already had.

When you are young, you tend to do so many stupid

things. It is a shame it takes so long for us to become smart!

Hockey and my full-time job kept me busy and Maureen had an outstanding job as a hairdresser in a local hair salon, and for years, we dated here and there, rather casually. That is, until a summer season or two ago, when despite my apprehension, our relationship became quite serious. That is indeed another entire adventure, but suffice it to say that our casual relationship would change quite a bit.

Eventually, Maureen Zipperelli knew that she could not compete for my heart with hockey, and she grew weary of waiting. She ended our relationship rather abruptly and without notice because of it. Maureen could no longer wait for me to put our love first, and she knew in her heart that hockey was too deep, too invasive in my soul and she did not want to be in second place any longer. I could not blame her; yet I could never muster the courage to tell her how much I cared for her or put her before my career dreams. One day, Maureen suddenly left forever, and a young man with his head screwed on tighter than mine was would never have allowed her to get away.

Now, upon closer examination, these career obsessions all seem to be a pattern with Paul John Henson.

"I am so glad that we could work out this date, Paul. Initially, when it took you forever to call me, I thought our little meeting that night was just a typical flash in the pan. You know, the handsome long-haired athlete that has his pick of the litters of women chasing after him, so I was just a passing fancy for you. I figured you were not interested at all. I know that sometimes, my aggressiveness and language turn men off. I know that we started off on the wrong foot that evening, but my ass sweetened up a bit from my first insults towards you. Didn't it?"

"Well, to say that you simply hurled a few insults my way, at least initially, to be honest, Renee, that could be perceived to be a bit of an understatement! However, to answer your question, yes, more than just your ass sweetened up towards me, yes, I do agree."

Renee smiled, but she did not comment or even chuckle at my subtle attempt at a joke. She seemed satisfied with my feedback.

I explained, "Honestly, hockey players are a different breed, Renee. We generally are not as if we are the star quarterback on the college football team, and no, I do not have litters of gals chasing me around the rink after the games."

"Shit, well, those women attending those games must be friggin' blind and dumb asses, Paul," she said with a coy smile.

"Please, Renee, not too many people ever call me, Paul. You may, of course, call me Paul if you choose to, but most people call me twenty-seven or they just call me, Paulie."

I towered over Renee Gorman while I stood next to her to hold the door open for her to climb into my jeep. She did not immediately answer my statement. In fact, Renee said nothing at all; she simply turned and smiled at me. She smiled that perfect smile, with those perfect, white choppers. She then nodded, clasped her purse in one hand, while folding the layers of her dress over her legs to allow her a seductive glide into the seat of the jeep with her other hand. I offered my hand out to help her, but she simply ignored my attempt at being a proper gentleman.

I would come to realize that this was typical Renee.

The first step on a jeep is straight up and quite high. Renee was short, but her height, for some reason, only added to her attractiveness.

To fly under her parent's radar, we had decided to meet over at the Ice Land Arena, which was my hockey home away from home, and as I had found out on the night when her car broke down, happened to be only a mile from Renee's home. It was a convenient location, and furthermore, I promised that if her car did not start, even if we had a spat, I would not leave her stranded.

Surprisingly, she enjoyed my dry humor.

Renee was a year older than I was, and as she had explained to me on the night that we met, she was a college student living at home and attending a local university. She also stated that while she was certainly free to make her own decisions, sometimes, it is just not worth the repercussions of such things.

On the telephone, while arranging this evening's date, I sensed her awkwardness in asking me to pick her up from the parking lot of the arena, and in essence "sneaking around" a bit. She felt she was alienating me, and to make her feel more at ease, I repeated to her again how I fully understood her position. She still lived under her parent's roof and on a daily basis; she had to deal with their wishes and opinions. There was no sense in rattling cages and causing a stir for no real reason. This relationship might be a passing fancy and would sputter after a date or two.

After all, we did not seem to have much in common. She despised hockey. We had very different religions, which were worlds apart, and I grew up lean and mean in the old neighborhood, while Renee lived upscale, in a fantastic home, with fine-trimmed lawns. It seemed as if this was just a passing fancy, and after a date or two, we would go our separate ways.

Maybe.

Once she sat down and settled into the jeep, I closed the door for her and scooted around to the driver's side. While I climbed into the jeep, I was about to find out once again that Renee Gorman might be petite, gorgeous, charming, and when she wanted to be, she could be very sweet, but she was indeed headstrong and she spoke exactly what was on her mind.

"Neither Paulie, nor twenty-seven, exactly turns on any romantic lights for me or sends any shivers down my loins, nor invokes any primal instincts. Therefore, I will call you,

Paul. You are too strong, tall and overwhelmingly handsome for Paulie, and twenty-seven does not mean too much to me. Seems a bit dumb to me, to be honest, as if you are hiding behind some false identity. I know it is your uniform number, your alias, a nickname per se, of your life as a hockey player, but I do not care much for sports. As you are aware of, and I do apologize, but I find hockey to be especially stupid. Bunch of stupid jackasses beating the living shit out of each other over a friggin' chunk of damn, hard-ass rubber and then trying to shoot a hole in your ass. All of this stupid bullshit is going on, while you stand in front of a hockey net, wearing layers of what has to be the most ridiculous equipment in all of the sports. At least football players wear some tight pants and the gals can check out their tight asses in the pants. You dressed in that get-up, who can tell what the hell you look like! Luckily, I met you out of uniform and could check you out."

I stood poised over the driver's seat with the door to the jeep open, and my body had not yet settled into the seat. I was staring at Renee, admiring her long speech and her amazing personality, trying hard not to smile or laugh.

Actually, I was not sure if I should laugh or cry.

I could tell that she was not finished with her thoughts because she shook her head; her earrings glistened in the darkness as her head moved. This woman was even gorgeous when she was tearing apart the one thing, other than my family and friends, that was most precious and important to me in my life.

Surprisingly, I did not mind in the least.

"Sorry, Paul. Hockey and everything about it are all kinds of dumb shit. Walking around with ice packs stuck up your ass and, on your body, all the time, and having to have your wounded ass all sewn up with a needle and thread."

Renee pointed towards a recently stitched cut on my forehead, which I had suffered in a game, and she used her pointer finger to emphasize her point. I fingered the cut and almost defended my honor by proclaiming how well it had healed.

I did not have a chance to speak because she took off again, voicing her forthright opinion.

"The sport is kind of brutish and barbaric. The ice-skating is cool. I do admire your abilities there. Other than the ice-skating aspect of the sport, it is all stupid nonsense. Well, not all of it is, other than giving you great muscles and a great build . . . hockey is bullshit."

She leaned back in the seat, smiled, and glanced over at me for my reaction. She seemed quite satisfied that she had so efficiently dismantled my hockey image and stated her honest opinion.

I had a feeling that stating her honest opinions in our relationship would never be any trouble at all for Renee Gorman. Her voice then grew soft and gentle, and a low rasp entered her intonation as she told me, "So you will be what you want to be, but in my eyes, I will always call you, Paul."

I did not know what to say. It was a magnificent diatribe. I must have looked quite dopey and slightly dumbstruck, as I slowly slipped into the driver's seat, nodded, and after pushing in the clutch and turning the engine on, I finally answered her, "Well now. Paul, it is then."

There was not too much more to say.

Our first date was to a local movie house to see a movie, and then we enjoyed a few drinks and a late-night snack at a nearby watering hole. I was a little nervous on this first date about making the correct impression with Renee. I was already behind the eight ball just a bit, my image working against me, but I felt that she was interested enough to agree to the date. Therefore, I wanted to do my best to impress her. Typical male ego stuff, but I kept my head out of the clouds; I still needed to be who I was. After asking around a bit, I decided that the usual watering holes that Harry and I frequented in and around Paterson, were not the types of joints that I wanted to bring Renee to, plus they were in the wrong geographic direction of where Renee lived. One of the players on my hockey club suggested a little tavern located close to the arena called, "The Gaslight Lounge."

It was perfect, not too expensive, not too cheap, quiet, lowlights and interesting décor. Since extra coins for me were always an issue, I was very pleased when the old man threw me an extra twenty-spot for the date. He noticed me, ready to leave for the date, dressed in a fancy black button-up shirt, black dungarees, my hair combed, beard trimmed, no hair tie, no sneakers, but instead, I wore a pair of black casual boots, polished (I could still shine them) to a mirror shine. No rock-and-roll tee shirts tonight!

"Looks as if ya fancied ya ass up tonight, Paulie. This new chickee-poo must be quite the dish. For ya to comb that hair of yours, bag the hippie bullshit and ditch the sneakers is a major step for ya to take. Looking good."

I smiled at my father's observation and thanked him. "Thanks, Dad. She is a nice gal, yup."

"Be safe and be smart. Here are a few bucks to take her to a nicer joint than those dumpy hockey gin mills that you and Harry hang out in."

He handed me the twenty bucks and shook my hand. I thanked him and was out the door in a flash. Pleasant surprise, but I was lucky. I had the best parents a young man could ever ask for.

It was a very pleasant date. Renee was talkative, opinionated, beautiful, and intelligent. I sat and stared at her, admiring her beauty in the lowlights of the tavern, her perfect features enhanced by the night, the atmosphere, and the conversation. Those golden earrings of hers, reflecting some light now and then, as she smiled and her head moved about. Gorgeous.

I did not speak too much, but interjected when I felt I should. Above all, I listened carefully to her every word and carefully studied Renee. She captivated me. Time passed by us so quickly; the waiter serving us, a short, jovial chap named Gary on the wait staff of "The Gaslight Lounge," gently reminded us of the last call, because we hung around until closing time. It was a wonderful place for a meal and a few drinks and I sensed that somehow, now, it was our place. The quiet table in the corner would now be our table, too.

Looking back, it was a magical conversation.

I was very comfortable around Jewish people. Our neighborhood was very diverse, and I was aware of and understood the culture. Renee did not speak with the usual New Jersey twang, nor did she speak with a traditional Northeastern Jewish accent. Eventually, it came out in the conversation at the watering hole over those same drinks that she was not a Jersey gal. She and her entire family were originally from Colorado, and her father brought the family to New Jersey about three years earlier, because of relocation for his employment with a large pharmaceutical corporation. He was some type of high-level executive in sales, and it was obvious that Renee was very close to her father and proud of him, too.

She laughed at my accent and certain words that I spoke in my New Jersey "speak," but she listened with great interest when I spoke a few words in Welsh, told her of my heritage, and why my New Jersey slang mixed in with the occasional, "Eh" and other British language nuances. She perked up when she heard of my background, and she enjoyed hearing of the meaning of the few words in which I could speak in Welsh. Renee was an English language major at her university; therefore, she was keen and focused on languages.

I told her of my mum and grandfather's failed efforts at teaching me, "Proper King's English," then she humored me by telling me that my accent was, "Not too bad."

Renee was taking courses locally at first, at a small independent university, while she felt her way through the curriculum. She looked towards the future positively, with a transfer of credits to a larger and more prestigious school, once she decided what exactly her future would be. She was very organized and methodical, and it was obvious that she had a simple plan.

"There is no sense spending a fortune on a basic education at some larger school, when I can work through the same courses here for less than a quarter of the tuition cost and save on room and board too. Besides, I can help my parents with upkeep on our home that once I move away from permanently, is entirely too big for just the two of them. I am an only child, and I am quite close to my parents—especially my father. They both work long hours and very hard hours, too. My friends required a college experience, they needed to get away from home, you know, parties, men, you know, stupid horseshit that you pay out of your ass for. I did not need that!"

Renee caught me off-guard when she gently motioned for me to clasp her hands. I was going to find out that she was quite adept at doing that and she could shift her personality from snarky to soft in mere seconds. She reached across the table, grasped my hands warmly, and looked deeply into my eyes.

Oh, boy, her eyes sure could sparkle!

"After all, Paul, I met a great guy right here. Almost next door."

I smiled, but I did not answer her. A change of the subject was in order, Renee seemed as if she was becoming romantic, and my comfort level with those types of conversations never fared very well. I needed to work on that aspect of my personality. Until then, instead, I asked her what her career aspirations were.

"Perhaps a teacher," she answered. But then again, she

was not too sure. "I have plenty of time to decide, Paul."

I agreed, because she certainly did.

She already knew of my career dreams, and she did not ask too much about ice hockey, and I stayed away from the subject. She already clarified that she was not a sport, or an ice hockey fan, and I actually felt it was refreshing to meet a person who did not dwell on my unusual career wishes. Hockey at times dominated my conversations and, in fact, my life. I felt that it was a nice change-up of sorts, to enjoy the company of a person who was less interested in what I was doing with my career, and focused more on Paul as a human, rather than number twenty-seven, the goalie.

There was no doubt that Renee Gorman was wonderful company. Despite my tendency to remain relatively quiet, when I did speak, Renee laughed at my dry humor; she held my hand warmly and generally seemed to enjoy the evening. I enjoyed being around Renee, and I think she felt the same about me, because when I said goodnight to her and asked her if she was available for another date, she emphatically answered, "Yes."

She gave me a warm hug when we parted that evening, surprisingly, there were no passionate kisses or even a peck on a cheek, or anything of the sort, and because of my affliction with the dreaded, "Old Lady Syndrome," I did not even attempt to steal a kiss from Renee, but it was obvious that there was an attraction.

Were there electrical sparks flying in the air and magnetic, passionate, genuine love at first sight? I was not exactly sure, but I thought so.

Our second date was a double date with Harry and Joyce. They both loved Renee, and she, of course, got quite a kick out of meeting the world-famous Harry M. Redmond Junior. Harry told me that I was crazy if I did not, well, you can imagine what he said.

There now was no doubt in my mind that there was indeed an attraction between Renee and me. We had a wonderful time on the second date, and then we had another date and another. . ..

Gradually, the goodnight hugs turned into goodnight kisses, along with a few passionate kisses mixed in here and there. Predictably, we had now claimed that quiet table in the corner of The Gaslight Lounge as our own.

The first change in our relationship and connection occurred one night on a date, about three weeks or thereabouts into our relationship. Renee and I were leaving The Gaslight Lounge, and we were walking to the jeep in the parking lot when a loud voice resounded from a dark corner of the parking lot.

I jumped, and turned around, as a man called out to Renee in a loud and cynical manner, "So, I thought that you hated hockey! Now, you keep company with a long-haired, hippie hockey player. A hockey player who is actually just a converted street thug too, or perhaps he is still one and that is the attraction. I would not think that to be your style. He is a few million miles beneath you, Renee, and he does not look Jewish to me!"

I turned around and instantly and instinctively pulled Renee close to me.

You see, I always protect my net.

I knew right away that this was the jilted boyfriend. I could have kicked myself in my own ass, for having too many stars in my eyes and not being more aware of this chap following us to track us down. That was a slipup of my keen training on the city streets, where you always needed to be aware of your surroundings. Renee put her hand on my arm, wrapped her other arm around my waist, and she held me very tightly.

She leaned in and whispered, "Easy there, my big goalie guy. That is my jack-ass ex-boyfriend, Byron Fielder. Forgive his comments and do not get yourself wound up too tight. I felt your muscles ripple. I can handle him. Please, please, please, just stay here. He is just a jealous jackass. He is a pre-law student and dumb as a bag of rocks. Can't pass the courses worth a damn. The dope has been a college student forever, and he is a hockey fan who thinks that he could actually be a hockey player. He does not understand what you could do to him because you would dismantle his sorry ass."

Typical, exact and factual, Renee Gorman.

Renee let go of me, walked over towards the man, I nodded as she turned towards me and mouthed, "Please" one more time to me. I stood next to the jeep and very carefully watched as Renee approached a man who emerged from the shadows and was still waving his arms rather emotionally as he spoke.

"Oh, so now you will talk! You will not return my phone calls, but now you will talk."

Renee stood next to him, and she spoke very softly and quietly. I could not hear what they were saying, but while it was killing me to follow Renee's wishes and stay where I was, it was obvious that Renee wanted to speak with him in private. He was taller than Renee was, but not by too much. He was a little on the heavier side for his height, weight, and frame, especially for such a young man. He wore a kippah skullcap. I noticed it right away and assumed that Byron, unlike me, was indeed Jewish.

The conversation remained calm to a point. I still could not hear too much, but when Renee went to walk away from him, Byron unexpectedly grabbed her arm and tugged at her, rather forcibly. When I saw that happen, I no longer followed Renee's wishes.

"No! Damn, now let go of my arm, Byron. It is over," was all I needed to hear, and in a mere second, I was standing next to Renee.

I reached to pull her in close to me.

"You need to listen to Renee. Let go of her right now and keep your bloody hands to yourself. I do think that this conversation is over," I announced.

He started to say, "I will do what I want and if that includes slapping her around. . .."

Byron saw the fire in my eyes, stopped in mid-sentence, looked up at me, and immediately let go of her arm. Renee tucked in tightly to me, and I gently guided her away from him and held her off to my side.

"What did you just say? Did you just try to say what I thought you said? Now, ya might just need to be measured for a coffin, pal!" Needless to say, I was angry because I thought Byron had begun to threaten Renee.

The little man became brave and spouted off, "Shit, don't think I am afraid of you just because you are some tough and rough ice hockey goalie. Drunk, I could have stopped the sorry-ass goal you let trickle in the other night. You suck in the net, your team sucks and everyone around here thinks you suck too. You are a small-time loser from the friggin' ghetto. You need a good haircut and a shave too. Sorry, lookin' hippie ass freak."

Byron pointed his finger at me. But he was smart enough to make sure that his finger did not come close to my chest. He could not reach my face.

He continued to spout off his frustrations, "My father is a high roller attorney. In fact, he is one of the most successful around here too and we could buy Renee a life, and everything that she could ever want in life. I read your biography in the game program. Telling some sorry ass sob story about how you made it to the Metropolitan Hockey League. Friggin' joke you are. Rollin' around town and that shitty city ya grew up in, inside some old piece of shit, rusty ass jeep. Surprised you took her to such a nice place to eat, ya must have had to do the dishes to pay for your meal, because you can't afford more than a can of cheap beer."

I smiled, as the words and lessons from that day so long ago at the Widow's Pub returned to me, "Always stand up for what is right and true, never back down when you need to protect your own, and always be true to your honor."

I stepped closer to him, and his eyes told me all that I needed to know, as he leaned backwards just a little. Funny how when truly confronted, some men are not quite as brave as when the malice-filled words are pouring out of their mouths. This chap and Mr. Davison had many things in common!

"I hope you feel better now after spewing a bit of boyish bullshit. As I have already told you . . . this conversation is now over. Moreover, until Renee tells you otherwise, then it will always be over. She controls her own thoughts and desires. Not you. I do not think you are quite as brave as you pretend to be, nor are you as tough as what you think you are."

I took a few steps closer to him while keeping Renee behind me. When I moved, he moved.

"I am sure you do not know or understand exactly what tough is. As far as your money and standing in high society by teaming up with your father and his position and earnings, then so be it. If that is the legacy that you desire, then go for it. I do need to warn you though, that guys such as I am, have no trouble at all in sticking silver spoons up pompous and pretentious people's asses. In fact, I will stick it so far up your dainty ass that it will be a little difficult for you to walk for a few weeks."

His eyes widened as he looked me up and down.

I now grew even more intense, "So Sherlock, you read all about me in a game program! Now, you are a damn expert on the subject of Paul John Henson. Besides, now, you have spoken some very brave words, especially brave words for someone who knows nothing about me, who I am, or where I have come from. All you have spewed has been supposition and jealousy, based upon poor observations. Sometimes, you need to be a man, face up to the world and have honor. Renee told you the story, punk-ass, now handle it, eh?"

He did not answer me, he just stared at me and his body language remained tense and taunt. He took a few more steps back and seemed thrilled to remain there.

"Now, my best advice is . . . that is, unless Renee asks you otherwise . . . she is her own woman, you know, that you leave her alone, stop trying so hard to make yourself big and other people small, and go and seek out some of your own honor. Otherwise, you will always be as miserable as you are right now. Good luck, pal. If you decide that you want to back up that big, brave, talk with action and you really believe that you are not afraid of this ghetto product, then when I turn my back to you and take Renee back to my jeep, then that will be your chance."

I now was angry and despite the anger, I knew that I needed to, as the old man had advised me, "Be Smart."

Looking deeply into his eyes, eyes that told me the entire story, I told Byron, "You need to heed a warning. I accept no free passes cuz you bit off more than you bargained for. Once you bring it—then I will finish it. So be forewarned there, little rich guy. If you still feel brave, then I suggest that when I turn my back, then you go for it. Just be sure to buckle your dainty ass in and bring your best game."

Putting my arm around Renee, I turned my back on him and led her to the jeep. I had no qualms at all, and I remained confident that Byron was not going to make any silly decisions at all this evening. I opened the passenger's door, Renee jumped in and when I walked over to the driver's side door and finally looked over to where he had stood, he was gone. I saw some taillights of a car ahead of us leaving the parking lot.

It was some high-end, fancy sports car.

"Are you, okay?" I asked Renee.

She smiled, leaned in close, and gave me the longest and most passionate kiss that we had ever shared.

"Of course. I am with you, mistah goalie guy. You take a lady's breath away, in so many ways."

Then, in typical Renee fashion, on the heels of incredible romance, she always had to have the last word and often it was a bit on the rough side.

"Told you, he was a jackass. Damn, stupid ass fool, he is! Following us around like some wild-eyed stalker. I must have had my head stuck in my own ass to have seen anything in him at all."

She looked at me with a glare in her eyes and smoke coming out of her ears. I knew better than to say a word or comment on her choice of men. I gently shook my head back and forth, made believe that I was buttoning my lips, and she laughed at my humor.

"You better not say shit, Paul, because I know what you are thinking. Byron is a big pussy, and he backed down, but I damn sure can kick your ass." I smiled, laughed, and took matters into my own hands. I gently pulled her in closer to me and kissed her deeply. Slowly, I felt her anger melt away.

From that night on, Renee and I were with each other every day, with the sole exception being when her class work interfered and I had either hockey practice or a game.

On those occasions, when we did not meet in person, we spoke on the telephone. That, in itself, was quite a change from my previous behavior because until now, I only ever spoke to Harry on the telephone, or I fielded the occasional work or hockey related telephone call. Those calls, typically, only lasted for a few brief minutes. My telephone calls with Renee, well, they lasted for hours. These calls were long, and that was much to the chagrin of the old man. My father constantly required the telephone for communications to the shop where he worked. He needed to work with the shop's maintenance team to nurse what seemed as if they were the world's most unreliable machines that broke down every few minutes. While I spoke to Renee, the old man would stand in front of me with his hands on his hips, waving his arms in the air, looking at his wristwatch, all to show that he needed me to hang up so that he could use the telephone.

When I asked Renee if I could call her back, because the old man required the use of the telephone, she in typical Renee fashion responded with, "Oh shit, tell him to hold on to his ass for a minute. Does he not understand that we are falling in love here on the damn phone? Tell him to tell that cheap-ass owner of the shop to spend a few bucks and buy some new damn machines!"

I am sure somewhere deep in the old man's heart, he had the same dream to tell the owner someday, the same, exact words and thoughts of which Renee just conveyed, however, in the best interest of everyone concerned, I did not relay that exact language to the old man. Instead, I rather diplomatically maneuvered my way around the precarious situation.

When Renee and I did not have schedule conflicts, and we went out together on dates, we typically had dinner, and some drinks, at our favorite table in the dark corner of The Gaslight Lounge, where the wait staff knew us well. We also enjoyed an occasional movie, but for the most part, we simply sat and talked at our table or in the jeep. We spoke for hours on end, speaking about most every subject that you could imagine. We conversed about our families, our friends, I told her of wild and crazy Harry and Paul adventures, she told me hilarious Jewish family stories of wild aunts, eccentric uncles and wonderful, loving, but overbearing Jewish grandparents. These were profound conversations of a rare and remarkable quality, two polar opposites in language, upbringing, culture and religions, yet the connection between us was undeniable.

One memorable date occurred upon a clear and starry night; we put the old jeep in four-wheel drive and climbed a backwoods trail to the top of scenic High Mountain in the nearby Borough of North Haledon. It was a spot in which Harry and I would often retreat to and discuss all of our troubles while sharing a bottle of whiskey, or two, or more bottles.

Renee and I parked, we climbed out, and we wrapped each other up in an old blanket that I always kept in the jeep. As I do recall, Renee always marveled at how the cold weather did not bother me.

She told me rather lovingly, in that soft, husky voice that seemed to change whenever Renee wanted to convey a special thought or two, "All you ever wear is that damn, skimpy vest. You are never cold. Hold me tightly, Paul. Wrap me in your arms and keep me warm and keep me safe as only you can do."

I think a magical part of Renee's allure and appeal was the manner in which she stood on her own two feet and projected a tough, solid, and strong exterior. At one moment, she was a woman who did not give a damn about anything or need anyone at all, but that was not always the case. I came to know that Renee Gorman could shift on a dime and become a gentle and romantic woman, leaning on her man for love and support. She was amazing in the manner that when she wanted you, she certainly made her feelings very clear.

That night on the mountain, together, we sat on the hood of the jeep. We passed a bottle of Scotch whiskey back and forth while we shared sips of it, and holding on to each other in the cool night air, in between, as the old man would say, "Swapping a few spits."

Crude description, but self-explanatory!

There we sat for hours, lying on the hood of the jeep, staring at the stars, while we admired the fantastic skyline of the big city that flickered in the darkness below us.

It was a wonderful view, and while we rested there together, we engaged in a remarkable conversation. I not only admired the stars in the sky and the beauty of the evening, but I admired the stars in Renee's eyes and her beauty too. I am not ashamed to say that as beautiful as the view was from the top of that mountain on that night, the beauty of Renee Gorman exceeded all of it.

She was a remarkable beauty, rare and intoxicating and as snarky as she could tend to be. She also could be soft, caring, gentle and oh yes, very sexy too!

"Paul, do you ever think of where your future is, other than wanting to continue to play hockey? I mean really think about the future. Think about your dreams, your desires, your life, whom you want to spend your entire life with and what it is that lies deeply inside of your heart."

"I think that I have, Renee. I know that hockey is not your bag, but besides that dream, I do think of what I would like out of life. Maybe a house, a few cars in the driveway, a lawn to mow once a week, some kiddies running around in the backyard. . .."

"No, no, no. Not that!"

Renee spun around under the blanket, and she held me tightly. She spoke in a whisper, a gentle tone, and I had to lower my head to look in her eyes while she spoke.

"For such a smart man, you can be such a dumb ass sometimes. Romance, Paul. Look the definition of the word up when you have a chance. I mean, what it means to be with one person and give them all of your heart. Have you ever thought about what it would be like to share all of those things with a special person? After I spend time or speak with you, it is as if I am floating on clouds. I have such energy, you bring me to a higher plane, a cheerful place and I am full of support and joy at simply sharing a conversation with you. On a deeper note, have you ever thought what it is like to lie together with someone, who you are in love with and with whom you have a profound connection, and together, you feel that not only your words and thoughts are in unison, but that your hearts are beating together in a perfect rhythm? Have you ever thought of that before?"

Renee stared intently at me and then she softly

whispered, "I have."

At first, I did not know how to answer. She had taken me by surprise and I never fared very well when it came to intense romantic discussions.

I answered honestly, "Those are beautiful thoughts, Renee. And no, to be honest, I have never thought of that before."

Renee pulled my face down close to hers and she gave me a long kiss. "Well now, mistah goalie guy, ya need to get your sweet ass in gear and start thinking about it . . . eh?"

Despite our remarkable connection and obviously growing romance, I longed to know exactly what Renee was thinking about me. She said we were falling in love, but had we arrived there yet? Was I that one person, of whom she was hinting about in her romantic speech? It was very hard for me to read the remarkable Renee Gorman. On the other hand, was it clear, and I was, as Renee said, "Being a dumb ass?"

She was quite unlike any other woman that I had been involved with or met before. With her rather poor opinion (to put it mildly) of ice hockey and for the most part, all sports, could she really love a hockey player? Did she and I have a special romance brewing here, or was it just a passing fancy? I felt that with the obstacles we faced with our many differences, the key question was, would we ever find a that we could have a future together and make a serious commitment to each other? I wanted to see if it would progress past discussing every subject imaginable and sharing warm moments of hugs, interlaced with occasional deeply passionate kisses and remarkable conversations. Then again, maybe this was a special love and, well, Renee's rather bawdy description of me was correct. I was a dumb ass.

There was an interest and a connection, however; were there going to be sparks between us? You know the feeling, weak kneed, dancing hearts, magical feelings about a special person, a smile on your face whenever you think about them. You go to sleep thinking of that special person and when you wake in the morning, they are the first person who you think about when you open your eyes. I had to ask myself, did an ignition of this relationship to bring it to the next step loom on the horizon? Were there going to be explosions and sparks?

About three months or thereabouts into our relationship, things changed a bit.

In fact, they changed quite dramatically. I found exactly the answers to what I required.

"I did not know that you were a fisherman!" Renee said rather excitedly, as she spotted my trusty old "collector's item" in the rear compartment of the jeep. She had reached into the back seat to place her jacket on the back seat of the jeep, and she spotted the old pole sticking out from the rear compartment of the jeep. It was late spring, almost summer now, but the evening air still held a bit of a chill. I had just picked Renee up from her university's parking lot for this date; amazingly, we still were not willing to risk a venture to the Gorman's house.

"Oh well, you never asked. Nevertheless, yes. I do occasionally go fishing. I have not been as often as I used to, hockey you know, it gets in the way of things. It is the off-season, but I am working hard to improve my skating. I stopped by a local fishing spot the other day and wet the line. Harry, Jeff and I used to fish quite a bit. Now, we are all so busy, but I still enjoy fishing now and then. It relaxes my mind."

"Are you kidding me, Paul? Why did you not mention fishing to me before? I love to fish! I see your old pole here. Are you a bait fisherman?" Renee asked as she examined my fishing pole. "This pole is awesome. It is so old, but it seems as if it has an incredible character." She leaned over the back seat now, and she rather closely examined the old pole. "Can I check it out?"

I must say, forgive me. But the view when she leaned over the back seat was quite spectacular. She wore a dress, thankfully, or perhaps in retrospect and frankly, not so thankfully! Renee wore her usual typical long dress; therefore, it did not reveal all the special gifts God had provided to her. However, it was bloody close.

Oh my, the view was still quite breathtaking.

That crazy Harry did have a valid point!

Suddenly, there were multiple explosions and sparks flew out of my heart.

Yes, we now had full romance lift off!

Apparently, we had much more in common than I thought.

"Of course, you may check it out. It is old, but very special to me. I have owned it forever and then some more. A long time ago, among some powerful lessons that I learned, I earned the money to buy it. And yes, to answer your enthusiasm, I am a bait fisherman, and as to whether I am kidding, well, as I said, you never asked me before. I had no idea that you enjoyed fishing. I would not have guessed that one in a million years."

She picked the old pole up out of the rear compartment and held it in her hands. Her eyes sparkled with lovely energy, and her face lit up in that fabulous smile. There was no doubt that her eyes could captivate you.

"Have you ever fly-fished?"

"No, I only ever had that pole and I never. . .."

Renee cut me off. She did have that habit, and I am always too long-winded and slow on the draw. She gently placed the pole in the rear compartment and babbled with a new enthusiasm that I had never previously heard from her.

"We will go! Let's go tomorrow. I have an extra fly rod and I will teach you to fly-fish for trout. You do have a license and a trout stamp, right, Paul?"

"I do. Yes, I do, Renee."

Renee gently replaced the pole in the rear compartment and then she climbed back out of the jeep and stood in front of me.

Smoothing her dress out, she smiled with an ear-to-ear smile as she said, "Wow! I was excited and bent over a bit with this dress on. I guess you were checking my ass out and dreamin' of future aspirations, huh? Tough shit, the dress was too long for you to see much there, mistah goalie guy!"

I tried hard not to be embarrassed at her correct allegations of my actions, and then decided that honesty was the best approach. Surely, my eyes had given me up, anyway.

Yet, as usual, my thick tongue stalled, and I took too long to reply, "Well, I do admit, Renee, that the view from here was quite. . .."

"Yeah, well, your time will come someday! I can only imagine what the muscles in your bare ass are like and what that naked athletic body looks like! Shit, hot sweat, Renee. . .."

Renee stopped in mid-speech, waved both of her hands at her face to mimic cooling herself down, and she laughed a little.

"Time to cool down and think about fishing. Yes, Renee cool down, girl, and think about only fishing and forget the fact that your panties are on fire."

She studied my face for a reaction, but I knew better than to say anything. Yet, her humor and mannerisms remained a remarkable aspect of her personality.

Bounding with enthusiasm, Renee shifted gears on the fly, "Can we go tomorrow? It is Saturday, so please tell me that you do not have to skate! I am sure you can take a day off from the ice to go fishing with me. Shit. You are already some kind of professional skater, one day off will not kill your ass. You ought to stick those skates up your ass occasionally to wake up and realize that there is more to life than hockey and work. We will pack a picnic lunch and go to a spot in Sussex County that my father and I used to fish at all the time. Please, please, please, Paul. I am so damn friggin' excited! It will be during Shabbat for us, but as I told you, I am my own woman, and I do not always practice what my family does. Besides, fishing is pleasure, and Shabbat honors pleasurable activities."

I thought to myself that for an English major, this gal has a heart of gold and the mouth of a hockey player. Furthermore, it was one of the first Yiddish words that I had ever heard Renee speak.

I must say that I was a little astounded here. Tonight, we had planned an extra special evening, which required me to dig extra deep into my wallet. We were going to The Gaslight Lounge. We planned to occupy our favorite table, and enjoy a special dinner that would be complete with a special bottle of Renee's fairly expensive and favorite red wine. There, in front of me, Renee stood, a soft, sweet, captivating young lady, gorgeous, dressed to the hilt while speaking of trout fishing. She even had a dainty and very elegant necklace of white gold hanging around her neck. The necklace matched her earrings perfectly, and it was the first time that I had ever seen her wear it.

I found it very difficult to believe that she was the outdoorsy type. She gave me no previous indication, and it was not something that I would have ever imagined within her personality or interests. Giving it a bit more thought, though, I recalled that she was from Colorado. Yes, of course, Colorado! I envisioned pristine Rocky Mountain streams, ice-chilly waters, teeming with trout and tumbling waterfalls. Very close to her father, fly-fishing . . . it all made sense now. Her father must be an avid fly-fisherman and taught his daughter the art of floating a fly. Even a dumb ass such as I was could connect the dots on this one. I bet she fished in a few spots, just a bit prettier than Molly

Ann's Brook and the Oldham Pond too!

While I stood there gazing at this gorgeous gal with the incredibly sparkling eyes, I quickly decided that I would be a fool not to answer, "Yes."

Therefore, I did.

I might have been many things, maybe a dumb ass, yes, but a fool was not one of them.

Chapter 3

I Would Love to Love You Once

Despite the extra special plans for the evening, the fancy bottle of wine, and Renee looking more captivating than any Hollywood movie star could ever look, we made it an early evening for our dinner date. It was not by my design. I actually had very little choice. Renee's zeal for fly-fishing had captured the night, and all she spoke about was fishing and how we needed to get some sleep, meet at her house early, we would try this nymph, and this wet fly and this dry fly, and so on and so forth.

It all meant very little to me.

I had once watched a television show that featured fishing and I had seen some chaps fly-fishing on some famous trout stream. Other than that, I was a total novice regarding anything other than drowning worms on the end of a hook. I mostly nodded my head and smiled in response to her conversation. She seemed to be an expert!

However, I examined the lick in her fabulous eyes, and I must say that the energy of her exuberance fully captivated me. I found myself amazed at her love of fly-fishing.

Wow! The last thing I would have ever thought to ignite our relationship would have been my old fishing pole. And, igniting it, we did. When I dropped her off and the evening ended, we shared a long and passionate kiss.

A special kiss that I am somewhat ashamed to say that

somewhere, or somehow, still lingers within my heart.

We met up at dawn on Saturday morning. The trout stream was about seventy-five miles outside of Paterson, and it would take us a bit of time to ride to, especially in my old rattlebox of a jeep. It was a coming of age of sorts; I was going to pick Renee up at her home! Renee told me at our special dinner on this now very special evening that she decided it was finally the correct time to tell her parents about our recent dating and all about me, too.

She planned her defense ahead of time, and she assured me that she had a well thought out delivery, "After all, Paul, I am an adult, free to make my own choices in life, you rescued my stranded ass from the parking lot and they are going to temple in the morning."

Who was I ever to argue with Renee Gorman!

That evening, after I dropped Renee off, Renee admitted to her parents whom she had recently been seeing. She called me later on that night and told me that all was well. Her parents were not overly pleased with her boyfriend selection; especially her father was particularly unhappy. Yet, Renee said, the fact that we were going trout fishing seemed to ease the pain of the Gorman's realization that their beloved daughter was keeping company with a long-haired, Lutheran, hippie, ice hockey goalie from Paterson. My assumption was correct in that her father was an avid fly-fisherman, and it was he who had taught his daughter the sport of fly-fishing. Fly-fishing made the cut; however, if Renee had told her parents of the dinner dates, drinks and movies, kisses, hugs and the love that we both felt growing within our hearts, then she might have had to live on-campus at her own expense for her final years of college.

I arrived early on Saturday in front of Renee's home, around four in the morning. Since it was so early, and the household was most likely sound asleep, I pulled alongside the curb of the home, rather than pull in the driveway. I did not want the noise of my old jeep's engine or the headlights to wake anyone. Especially her parents!

Renee must have been watching for me, because I barely had stopped the jeep and shut the engine off, when the front door to her home opened and she appeared in the doorway. I could clearly see her silhouette framed by the dim glow of the lights in the foyer of her home. She waved to me with an indication to come and assist her with carrying the tackle and assorted gear.

"Hello. Bore da, Renee."

"Bora' your ass, Paul. I have no time to figure out some gibberish Welsh bullshit right now. Grab this stuff before my parents wake up and they change their minds about you. My father also hunts occasionally. Warning, because he can shoot a rifle almost as well as he can fly cast. We can snuggle later, right now, hustle that tight little ass of yours and load your jeep. Take these fly rods, those wader boots, that bag over there, and that cooler. I have the rest of it. I staged this stuff ahead of time, so we can book out of here quickly."

"Okay, well—then let's go!"

I was not going to argue, nor was I going to test any waters and linger. As far as her father's accuracy with his aim, I decided just to take her word for it and not to experience any details of it.

Before I knew it, the jeep was loaded, and we were, too. Renee was seated in the jeep, fiddling with the lid of a thermos of coffee, and we were rolling north on the interstate. She leaned over, kissed my cheek and smiled at me, while she handed me a steaming cup of coffee poured straight from the thermos, along with some type of pastry. I had not eaten anything since last night's dinner, so I gobbled a bite of it. It was delicious. I had no idea what it was, other than some type of Jewish pastry of some sorts, but it sure tasted good.

"Don't pucker your little Lutheran ass up worrying

about it. Yes, it is all kosher. Pareve," she told me with her sarcastic chuckle that I was now very accustomed to. Now, I knew that she was Jewish, she took care of everything, especially any culinary or kitchen related items!

Renee was dressed in a heavyweight, black, plaid flannel button-up shirt, covered in a presently unzipped woolen vest, with a pair of tight dungarees on, which clung to her amazing figure as if she had painted them upon her body. The ever-present white gold dangling earrings remained; I could see the sparkle of them as she moved her head in the dim light of the early morning and the interior of the jeep. It was the first time that I had ever seen her without her trademark dresses or skirts on, and I thought how this woman could wear a burlap sack and look stunning.

Perhaps she observed me checking her out, or it was just that peculiar, yet amazing Renee Gorman intuition, but between sips of coffee, she glanced over at me and commented in her remarkably candid manner, "I look hot, huh? Even in the dim light of this crummy jeep, I see you checking me out! Well, I am hot in looks, but cold as shit! Paul, damn! I am freezing my ass off in here!"

Out of the corners of my eyes, while I tried to lock my eyes on the roadway, she stared me down while I smiled at her comments. Oh, oh, she was not finished yet. She launched off in a typical, long Renee speech.

"As usual, you look amazingly hot. You are hot all over, but your cold-blooded ass is a major pain in my ass. You're never cold! Must be from living in those dingy, shitty ice rinks! The temperature must be in the twenties early this morning. There you sit, all happy and cozy, while annoying the hell outta me, wearing no coat, just a vest on your skinny ass, canvas sneakers and a rock-and-roll tee shirt. You really do not dress to impress, Mr. Henson. Do you?"

Renee leaned back in her seat for a brief minute, zipped up her vest and she folded her arms across her chest. Then she glanced my way for an answer.

At first, I shrugged my shoulders because I knew that my answer would be way too long-winded for Renee, and she was feeling snarky. Even though I already knew my fate, I opened my mouth and decided to give it a whirl anyhow, "Well, I never. . .."

Predictably, Renee took off again.

She was not going to wait for my long-drawn-out explanation.

"Oh well, when you look as good as you do, then I guess you can get away with it. Are you not cold? Cuz, my ass is freezing. Do not get all hot and wacky on me now, but my nipples are like darts! Turn the damn heat up on this old piece of shit jeep! Will you please?"

I immediately reached for the dashboard knobs and turned them all to maximum. There was little doubt that heat might be a farfetched dream on my old jeep, but I could try. As far as the rest of the reply to her comments, I wisely steered clear of them. But there was no doubt that someday, I needed to upgrade my attire.

Besides, she looked amazing.

Renee spoke in excited waves the entire ride to the trout stream, and in between speaking; she pointed and barked out road directions. For not being a native New Jersey resident, she sure knew the roads well enough. I suspected that she had charted these roads with her father quite often. The roads seemed as if they were unforgettable to Renee, and most likely, were associated with some very fond memories.

We made a left turn off the main interstate, rolled into a long ramble down a dark, wooded and winding road, then a made few turns more, and Renee proudly announced for me to pull into a wooded turnaround, while she said, "We are here!"

Here? Where? All I saw was a slight clearing in the woods and the remnants of what could be a road . . .

maybe. Good thing that I had a jeep.

"You will need to put this wreck into the four-wheel drive. The spot is secluded, and the road is actually not a road, but a narrow path. A jeep will make it—even this jeep."

"This jeep is tougher than you give it credit for," I said while I jumped out of the jeep, locked the front hubs, climbed back in and slipped the transfer case of the jeep into a four-wheel drive low gear. I eased the clutch down and shifted into gear while the jeep easily crawled up a wooded embankment to a little ridge overlooking a pristine stream.

The sun was licking the horizon now, and I could hear the water of the trout stream tumbling down the rocks and crevices below us. The colors of the sunrise were amazing, with bands of yellow, red, and some golden colors, which worked from the eastern ridge, to the zenith of the sky above us, chasing the moon and stars away as the night reluctantly gave way to the day.

I shut the engine off, leaned back in the driver's seat and thought about how people whom only traveled up and down the New Jersey Turnpike, did not understand the genuine beauty hidden within my glorious home state.

Renee did not linger and admire the sunrise; instead, she popped out of the passenger's door of the jeep and she literally ran over to the driver's side. Bursting with energy, she swung the door of the jeep wide open, leaned in and kissed me passionately.

"Damn, a coffee-laden kiss. Sexy as hell. Now, let's suit up, might be a nymph hatch going on right now."

"A what?" I asked, much preferring to try another coffee-laden kiss. Trout? What trout? What the hell is a trout? After a kiss like that, under the glorious sunrise that we were experiencing, with clear tumbling waters below us and a gorgeous woman for company, I was not ashamed to say that a damn trout was the last thing on my mind.

I climbed out of the jeep and stood in awe as I watched this beautiful, petite young lady dress into a pair of hip waders, put on a fishing vest, and magically transform before my eyes, from a gorgeous, petite young woman, into a walking advertisement for a fishing gear company. I must say that she looked as beautiful in hip waders as I imagined that she did in an evening gown.

The entire time that she dressed, Renee rambled on, "I cannot tell you how wonderful this is. It has been so long since I have been here at this stream. My father and I used to fish this part of the river all the time, but he has been so busy at work these days. He received this big promotion, and the stress and long hours are so difficult. I have school now. You know the situation, Paul. We just do not have the time."

She looked up at me and through the early morning light filtering down through the trees, I could see the reflection of her smile. Even her earrings sparkled a bit. I still said nothing, just a nod of my head; I was too much in awe of her to move.

I must have looked like a dope.

Off she went on one of her patented, long diatribes, laced with her colorful language, "Well, shake your ass, goalie guy. Hungry trout await our efforts. It is cold now, but as soon as the sun is higher, it will warm up and I bet a little insect hatch will occur. It is almost June now, and I am willing to bet that no one has fished this part of the river since early May. Everyone gives up too early when it comes to trout. Those hip waders in the back of the jeep should fit you. They are my father's extra pair. He is not half as tall as you are, but he has enormous feet, so I bet you will fit in them nicely. I would offer you a hat and fishing vest, but I know you will not wear them. You have to be all manly-man on me, or some kind of stupid shit like that. I will take another coffee-laden kiss though."

Before I knew it, we had climbed down a steep bank;

made our way to the stream, and we were both standing knee-deep in the stream while we were casting wet flies, known as nymphs, into the quiet pools below a small waterfall.

To be honest, Renee was casting the flies.

I was mostly clearing tangles in my line and pulling the fly line leader out of my long hair. This fly-casting business was not too easy. Where was my collector's item? It was a lot easier to hurl a worm into the water than toss the fly whoosie that had no weight to it at all!

Renee gave me a few quick lessons on how to fly-cast; she laughed at my feeble efforts and used her usual colorful language to describe my rather inept fly-casting talents. Finally, she decided the best method for me to learn was for her to show the correct technique to me. I paused and watched in awe as she gracefully and elegantly laid a long rolling cast of her fly line out towards the waterfall, and the fly effortlessly landed in the swirling green waters of the rapids. There, the current would naturally drift the fly along the streambed where a hungry trout would see it while they faced towards the current, looking for their next meal. I stood and watched, and on about the sixth cast, I saw her smile when her line went tight. She had a fish on!

"Wow! That was quick! I think you have a trout on!" I shouted as I watched her effortlessly pull the line taunt and then peel some extra line from the reel to allow the trout to run and tire out a bit. The fly leader lines were tiny; we were using around a one-x tippet. Too quick of a tug and you would lose a fish and a fly too!

Renee turned, smiled, and yelled out, "I see that you are still a damn genius, Paul!"

She was amazing, and I licked my wounds for my stupid observation while she played the fish carefully out of the rapids. I could tell that another sly comment was coming; she had a certain look that I was now familiar with whenever she wanted to tease me a bit.

"Yes, well, when you actually can get your line and fly into the water and not tangled in long locks of golden curls, or stuck up your ass, then you have a chance of catching trout!"

"Point well taken, there, Miss Professional Fisher Lady. I can take it, and while I admit to having the line tangled in my hair, well, as far as stuck up my ass, no not yet at least."

"Give it time. I have no doubt in your remarkable abilities, Paul. Oh, Paul, come over and check it out. It is a brookie. Might be a native. Just look at the fabulous colors!"

I carefully waded over to Renee, being mindful of the moss on the rocks, which was very slippery. I stood next to her and watched as she expertly held the fly rod high in the air, unclipped a trout net from her belt and netted the brook trout.

She smiled as if she had just won a million dollars.

What a smile and what a scene. It was the most amazing display, this petite, gorgeous woman who was an expert fly-fisher lady.

Bloody amazing.

I leaned over, studied the fish, as Renee held the fish in her hands, and gently worked the nymph out of the corner of the trout's mouth. It was around ten inches or so in length, a little fat, and the colors were deep and remarkable in the sunlight. One of God's grand creations, and the colors were breathtaking.

"Gorgeous colors, and as you would say . . . I will add an, eh."

"It is beautiful, Renee. Almost as gorgeous as you are, eh?"

At first, she ignored my effort at a romantic compliment, but once the nymph was loose and she gently slipped the fish back into the water to set it free again, she looked up at me.

"The fun is in catching them and not killing them.

Almost as gorgeous, but not quite, eh?"

"No, actually, in all honesty, nowhere near. . .."

"Well, even though you added a stupid eh in the sentence just to piss me off, mistah goalie guy, you just earned a kiss. Now, it is time for me to be honest, because I need to wipe my hands of fish goo on your shirt, so wiggle your ass on ovah here."

She set her fly rod down upon a rock. I did the same, we shared a long, wet kiss, and yes, she did in fact, wipe her hands on my shirt. Renee Gorman only ever spoke the truth, and she spoke what was exactly on her mind.

It was worth it.

There was something very unusual about fly-fishing on a trout stream and sharing a passionate kiss with a gorgeous young woman. It was a situation in which I would never have imagined in a million years and a long way from sitting on the banks of that chemical infested brook with Jeff and Harry.

Let us just say that the scenery, in many ways, was a whole lot better looking!

"So, the score is the good Jewish girl, one trout, and the hippie, Lutheran, professional goalie guy, has caught, shit. Zero . . . zilch. In fact, you have yet even to land a fly into the water."

She pointed dramatically at the stream and motioned with her hand while pointing a finger towards the water.

"Paul, hint, hint, hint, you need to put the fly into the water, because that is where the fish live. Catch a trout, you earn a kiss, catch a few more and who the hell knows what your handsome ass might earn!"

She winked at me seductively, and between her beauty and her sarcastic sense of humor, I could tell that I was falling even more deeply in love with her. She was snarky, alluring, romantic and tough, all in one package.

Bloody amazing.

I thought, well now, a hint at romance and a challenge.

There is nothing that number twenty-seven enjoys more than a challenge. I live for them.

"Yeah, yeah, yeah, a challenge, eh? I am an athlete, ya know. Goalies deal in challenges all the time. Don't say that I did not warn you!"

"That is what I am counting on," she said as she sat down on a nearby rock, tucked her fly rod under her arm and with her other arm, she waved across the stream as if to show that it was all mine to try.

I waded out into the rapids and took a deep breath. Geez, this cannot be that bloody hard to do. After all, I am a professional hockey player. Think of your training. The goalie stick is an extension of my arm; therefore, the fly rod is an extension of my arm.

Mechanics, motions. . .. C'mon, Paulie! I mean, c'mon, Paul.

A few waves of the fly rod, followed by a carefully timed release of the line, and, and, and, the fly went straight up into the air. I ignored the giggles emitting from behind me. A few more attempts and more flies that went nowhere. In fact, one fly stuck in a shrub behind me, and I had to wade out of the stream and unhook it.

Renee offered no assistance at all in unhooking my errant cast. She sat observing the scene of my struggle while perched on the edge of a rock. She was now wearing her sunglasses, posing and looking gorgeous, while snickering at my feeble fly-casting attempts. On what seemed as if it were the seventy-seventh thousand, and second cast, I finally landed the fly into the water cleanly. Renee stood up and cheered, and she clapped wildly. She always told me that she loved my dry humor, but her humor was not too shabby either.

It was so much fun to laugh with her.

When you search the world over and find someone who can make you laugh, perhaps, a little bit at yourself, and at one another, then you have found a rare and precious gem.

She cheered even more wildly when that first successful cast landed a little brook trout!

When I successfully brought the fish to the edge of the stream and together, we admired it.

Renee playfully whispered, "Mine was bigger and the colors on my trout were prettier too."

I did not care because it earned me a kiss and at least I did not have to have fish goo wiped on me. For a brief second, I pretended as if I was going to wipe my hands on her shirt. But that was a horrible idea.

"No way, mistah goalie guy. No fish goo on me while you try to steal a free feel of my chest. Wipe the fish goo on your own ass."

What a pepper pot Renee Gorman was.

We fished the morning away. Laughing, smiling, and talking about every subject on our minds and then some more, all while enjoying the fresh air and the glorious day. The sun climbed higher and higher in the sky and soon it was warm and enticing on our backs.

I mostly stood in the stream, just watching and admiring Renee Gorman, finding myself thanking God for creating such beauty, such a glorious person, a goddess.

We each caught fish. Renee had a total of four trout caught and I had three, and with the daily limit in New Jersey, being six per day, we still had some trout to catch. We might have fished out the deep pool under the waterfall because the action came to a halt. Either we had caught most of the trout there or spooked the rest under the rocks, therefore after one-half an hour or so of no nibbles, we decided to work our way downstream.

Renee knew of another hotspot a few clicks downstream and we moved along the bank towards a deep pool, several hundred yards south of where we began fishing.

As we moved along, I studied Renee's eyes as she watched the rolling river rapids, and she tried to recall the spot in which she was searching for amongst the tumbling waters. Even underneath sunglasses, I could see her dark eyes sparkling and I felt that their appearance today was especially captivating; as if the beauty of her eyes could penetrate the darkness of the lenses.

"Here, Paul! Yes, this is a good spot. Right over here where the river bends and curls. The stream changes from fly-fishing only to bait fishing after those bends and curls, anyway. You could go get that old ass pole of yours and use it over there. That is, if the son-of-a-bitch still works. Let's move out here. I think this is the spot," Renee explained as she pointed and waved for me to follow her as she suddenly peeled off the bank of the river and she quickly moved out into a deep stretch of quiet, slow-moving water.

It seemed as if she was eager to fish this section of the stream, and she was moving along rather quickly.

The Old Lady Syndrome and some instinct of pending danger crept into me. I was watching her rather hastily navigating along, while inside, I was mustering up enough courage to warn the professional fisher lady that the rocks had thick coverings of moss all over them. I wanted to shout out for her to be careful, and before my usual long-winded mind could produce the words, Renee stepped rather confidently upon a large, rock edge to move to the north end of the pool and it happened!

I watched in horror as her normally graceful body slipped off the rock and she went tumbling, head over teakettle, into the stream!

"Renee! Geez! Oh, geez! Damn! Shit! I am on my way!" I tossed my fishing gear aside and hurried to reach her.

I could move fast!

I was frightened for her safety, and I feared the worst of situations.

I had no way to gauge how deep the water might have been and how strong the current was! In addition, Renee could have struck her head upon a rock, and with hip waders on that could fill with water. This was an awful scene. My heart raced. I took giant leaps and bounds and jumped through the water and leaped over rocks and ledges. I was there in mere seconds, scrambling over the same rock that caused her to tumble into the river, leaping and jumping to reach her. Thankfully, it turned out that my fears were for naught. The water where she tumbled into was a slow-moving pool with no rocks in sight, and the water was only about two feet deep or so.

Renee disappeared under the water for only an instant. I had already reached her in seconds and my arms grabbed her petite body, and I pulled her clear, up, and out of the water with a powerful grasp. I held her up and embraced her, holding her closely and tightly to make sure she was safe and unhurt.

She was okay, but she was soaked!

After shaking her head and spewing a string of obscenities that still linger over New Jersey to this very day, she laughed uproariously. She was soaked head-to-toe.

"Are you okay? Are you hurt? You did not hit your head or anything else, did you? You scared the living daylights out of me!"

Renee shook her head, wiped the water away from her face, her short hair dripping water over her eyes.

She smiled and between laughs she said, "I am fine, I am not hurt, a little cold and certain parts of me have shrunk and others are rock hard, if you know what I mean, but I am fine. Only my pride is hurt. Here I am, all cocky and self-assured, and I go on my ass into the water. Where is my fly rod? My gear? Did I lose my damn sunglasses? Wait, no, no, no. I put them in my bag before I fell on my ass."

I looked her over and told Renee, "I have the fly rod and your bag is on your waist along with your net. I think you have it all, nothing was lost, except as you said, perhaps, a bit of your pride."

She stopped laughing. I pointed towards the shore, held her tightly and as we waded carefully back to the shore and we carefully avoided that same rock. I could feel her attitude soften.

There were many facets to Renee Gorman's personality, she could be hard, she could be soft, she could be introspective, but I could tell by her touch on my arm, and how she held me around the waist right now, she could be full of love too. We reached the shore and even in the bright sunlight; she was now shivering, and she motioned for me to lean down and kiss her. It was a deep kiss, powerful, very different from all of our previous kisses. Something had seriously changed between us.

I could feel it and I knew that so could Renee.

She whispered to me while I held her, "You care deeply. You are amazing. I cannot believe how quickly you jumped into the water to grab me. No regards at all for your own safety, whatsoever. Fearless. Thank you for caring, for noticing me, as no man has noticed me before."

We kissed again, and I whispered, "Only a blind man or a fool would not be able to notice you, Renee Gorman."

Then, in typical fashion, she had to shift gears from being soft Renee, to well, being Renee, "I love how tall and strong you are. It is wonderful, but it is a major pain in the ass, how hard it is for a person of my height to reach those lips of yours, otherwise, I would wear them out right now, Paul John Henson."

She could never let me ride easily for more than a few very brief minutes. There was never any sense in ever becoming comfortable when Renee Gorman was around.

She shivered and now I grew concerned because Renee was going to require warmth very soon. I kissed her one more time and thought of a plan. My arms around her were not enough to warm her and now I was wet too.

"Well, you are in luck, Renee. As a certain friend of mine

named Harry M. Redmond Junior always painfully reminds me, as a hapless victim of the dreaded Old Lady Syndrome, I have a solution to getting you warm, rather quickly. We need to return to the jeep."

Renee nodded in agreement while she shivered some more.

I did my best to hold her tightly while juggling all of our fishing poles and gear, and we started the long walk back to the jeep, staying in the warm sunlight in a vain effort to stop her shivering.

While we walked, I tried my best to keep her warm, and I explained, "Due to the fact that all of our lives, my old man and now, I, all have driven junky and unreliable vehicles, I am of course, prepared. I have in the rear compartment of the jeep, in addition to the toolbox of which you are already acquainted with, a warm woolen blanket."

Renee looked at me and between shivers; she waved her hands in the air in a signal to get to the point. She had little patience right now. In fact, most of the time, for my extended explanations.

"You will recall that it is the same blanket which we used to stay warm with on that night on High Mountain. I also have a large woolen mat. You see, when you have to sit and lay your body down on the side of the road, on a freezing cold night to make emergency repairs on junk vehicles, then you bring along the correct equipment. The mat prevents you from freezing to death while on the ground swinging wrenches, and the blanket, well, I always kept it just in case I could not get the jeep rolling again and I had to sleep in the jeep on the side of the road. My old man taught me well."

Renee looked over at me. And because she did not wear her sunglasses, her eyes squinted a bit in the sunlight, but she did not comment. More accurately, she did not comment right away; yet, knowing Renee, I knew she was working up the correct insult to let me have it at just the precise moment. She required just a little more information to load her verbal cannons with the correct sarcastic charges.

I continued to prove why I was such a victim of the Old Lady Syndrome, "I also have in my hockey equipment bag, a Long Island Rooster tee shirt, an extra set of clean warm-up practice pants, a few thermal undershirts, which I use under my jersey and practice jerseys. They are all fresh back from the laundry, believe me, you would not want to be near them after a practice, but these are all fresh and crisp. After all, someone had to be prepared for when any professional fisher persons go on their gorgeous asses into the ice-cold river!"

I smiled and looked over at my shivering companion. I could tell by the look on her face and the lick in those fabulous eyes that she now had all that she required in order to let me have it.

Yes . . . here it comes!

She gave me a strong, playful push-off with both of her arms and blasted me, "So, I have a gorgeous ass, eh?"

"Ah yes, you do."

"Ha! Checking my ass out will get you nowhere, mistah goalie guy. Playing all innocent like while checking out my ass. I think that you have taught old Harry a few more things regarding young ladies than you will admit. Regardless of your lewd behavior, Harry is correct. You are a damn old lady. You suck! What a pansy-ass you really are. Big, tough, rough, goalie guy, who is like a little forest scout in the woods, with all of his tools, blankets, his reference book and emergency kit. All prepared for emergencies. You are so damn efficient."

I laughed and grabbed her tightly again, while whispering, "I don't have a reference book. I keep it all in my head."

"I am not wearing damn hockey shit! I hate hockey. The

thermal and warm-up pants are okay, but I'll be damned if I am wearing that stupid jersey you wear with some dumb-ass looking duck on it."

"It is a rooster, Renee, not a duck."

"Whatever! Stupid ass lookin' logo. How rough and tumble is that? Stupid bullshit! A bunch of friggin' roosters skating around on the ice."

I almost said what was on my mind; that we could call a rooster by another name, which would be a bit manlier. The words moved from my mind to my lips as we prepared to climb the steep bank from the river to the jeep, but Renee stopped and stalled in front of me.

She put on her brakes. Her mind was too sharp and snarky to miss it.

She waved her hand at me and said, "And don't say it. That we also know a rooster as, a–you-know-what! Smart-ass. I can tell by those eyes of yours, what you are thinking. You're not quite the innocent Old Lady Syndrome victim all the time, are you? Your eyes give everything away about you, Mr. Henson. You would make a shitty secret agent, even with your English background, and handsome, smiling ass."

"I am not considering a career change at the moment, but as far as the rooster goes, well, the thought crossed my mind."

"Sure, it did. I knew what you were thinking."

"Do you know what the definition of a smart-ass is?"

"No, but I am sure that I am about to find out."

"It is someone who can accidently sit on a scoop of ice cream and tell you what flavor it is."

Renee smiled, chuckled, and said, "You are such an old lady. Good thing that your marvelous sense of humor does not rely upon telling jokes, but that was not a bad joke for an old lady. You are handsome, but such a damn cornball. I admit, that is a very intelligent ass though, and quite profound and funny. Speaking of asses, my pants legs are soaked inside of these waders. I cannot even lift my legs to take this first step up the rocky bank here. Put your enormous hands on my beautiful wet ass and give me a push, will you. I will grant you a free squeeze."

Well, now, this job I could handle.

We reached the top of the bank, and with air temperatures in the mid-fifties, I knew that it was time to put aside the playful kidding and bantering. Renee required warmth, and despite the bright sunshine, she still was shivering dramatically, even more so than she was previously.

I ran ahead to the jeep and dropped the fishing gear on the ground next to it. I unsnapped the rear soft-top cover, revealing the storage compartment, and I called out to Renee, "I could turn the heat on, but as you already know, the heater does not throw enough heat to be worthwhile. Here, let me get the blanket and the mat, and the dry clothes. You can toss the mat upon the ground and stand on it so that your bare feet are not on the rocks. I can look the other way or you go down the hill, you can cover up with the blanket and change into. . .."

I stopped speaking and turned around when I heard Renee begin to speak. I did not realize that she had run alongside me and now was standing directly behind me.

"What in the hell are you rambling on about, Paul? I am not hiding in the woods, like some damn, naked ass bear. I am freezing to death, and there is no other person around for friggin' miles. Please, toss the mat on the ground right here next to the jeep, give me the blanket, stop talking like some stupid fool and get your ass on over here."

Renee paused and her voice changed to a serious tone while she waved for me to hurry.

"Please hurry, Paul. Seriously, my ass and everything else on my body are freezing."

When I saw her, I stood there a little dumbfounded, in fact, a little sheepish, while still holding the blanket and mat in my hands. Now, the word dumbfounded might not be the correct word to use, perhaps the word awestruck works better.

She smiled and shivered while she stood there, stripped down to her brassiere and panties. Her erect nipples on her amazing breasts clearly showed through the cloth of her brassiere, and I could see the outlines of the gently groomed hair of her pubic area through the clinging cloth of her wet panties.

Her body was perfect, her olive skin glowing, perfect curves, perfect breasts, perfect hips, and legs. Perfect. Beyond perfect. Flawless. Renee was a gorgeous goddess.

I handed her the blanket and laid the mat down upon the ground as my heart raced at the sight of her.

"What's wrong? Have you never seen a girl in her underwear before, big tough, mistah goalie guy?" Renee asked while she took the blanket from my hands and wrapped herself up in it. I saw her shiver and grab the wool tightly as she hugged the warmth out of it. I still did not answer her, but she waved gently for me to come closer, and I did so without even the slightest hesitation.

Old Lady Syndrome . . . eh?

What, Old Lady Syndrome?

As I moved closer to her, Renee opened the blanket up and while we embraced, she pulled the blanket around both of us. Her voice changed dramatically. It was different now. It was soft, deeper, and full of seduction and warmth, and the look in her eyes was even darker than usual.

I knew what that look meant.

As I said, I was many things, but a fool was not one of them.

"Your shirt is soaked from my missteps of foolishness. Here, lift your arms and pull it off. We will restore each other's warmth and perhaps even venture where we will warm each other's hearts too."

I pulled my shirt off, and I tossed it aside; she studied

my bare chest for a long time while she slowly and gently ran her hands up and down it. Her eyes were intense and I could feel her chest moving up and down, as her breaths were deep and strong. I pulled her in close and our bodies molded together in perfect unison. Her ample breasts tucked tightly against me and her nipples were hard and pointed through the thin layer of the cloth of her brassiere.

I could feel her heartbeat upon my chest.

"My, my, my . . . hockey is good for something other than scars and pain. You have a remarkable body, Paul. Chiseled into perfection. An athlete's body. Damn, what muscles. Yet, you are so soft. My loins are aching now. There are shivers going up and down my body, and it is not from being cold anymore. You are marvelous. Even more so than my imagination could envision. I had no idea . . . what this would be like, what it could feel like, until now."

I locked into her eyes while we kissed and she locked into mine. Right from the first glance, it was that way with the two of us. Our eyes met and our eyes told the entire story. Before I knew it, we gently fell upon the mat on the ground and while her breathing changed to deep gasps, she anxiously fumbled with the belt on my pants and soon she was fully unclothed, and I was too.

She was indeed a goddess. A woman of rare and intoxicating exquisiteness.

She whispered to me, "Please excuse my truthfulness, but I have to tell you that I have never been fully with a man before, but I would love to love you once. I can think of no one who I would rather it be with, other than you, Paul John Henson."

My heart pounded, my inhibitions left, and I felt a deep love for this woman. There was no way that I could have allowed this to happen if it was anything other than remarkable love that I felt for her. We had only known one another for a relatively short amount of time, yet I knew she was rare and precious. We were such polar opposites, both in culture, religion, upbringing, language, and emotions, but in many ways, we were so much alike.

Maureen Zipperelli and I had shared a very special relationship over several years, and during that time, we eventually shared each other's bodies several times, too. Actually, to my own surprise, I was an experienced lover, and I was very intuitive.

Renee and I shared each other's love, as well as every inch of each other's bodies, for the entire rest of the afternoon.

It was needless to say that Renee warmed up quite a bit and so did I.

There were golden flashes of light all around us. There was joy, and there was indescribable passion. The trembling of our bodies and the combined beating of our hearts seemed as if it shook the very ground underneath us. At one point, we held each other, exhausted and gasping for air.

Renee whispered in my ear, "Quiet, Paul. Try hard to stop breathing so deeply for a second. Do not say a word. I want to remember this moment forever. Can you feel it? It is just as I had dreamed that it would be."

She gently placed her hand on my chest, and she took my hand and placed it on hers, just above her glorious, bare breasts.

"It is magic, Paul. Our hearts are beating together in a perfect rhythm. How I wish that the power of our love could stop the sun from setting and that this day would never end."

We stopped making love, only to enjoy the lunch that Renee packed for us. Then we started honoring our love again and finished the day wrapped up in the blanket on the ground. I think exhaustion finally set in and we fell asleep for a long time, because I recall that when we awoke, the sun was glowing just above the horizon in the western sky.

It was a golden sunset, which mixed with red and some blue hues . . . colors, which sublimely broadcasted that the end of the day was here. Nighttime would soon chase this fantastic day away, and with it, there would be some extraordinary memories.

Yes indeed, the day ended, and what a day it was. When you are young, you are innocent, and if you have inhibitions, you tend to tread carefully along the precarious ridges of your heart and of your soul. There is forbidden love, and star-struck lust, however, in some rare cases; there is inevitable love, which I think is really true love of sorts.

The chance meeting of two people that for whatever reason, fate joins together, to share something special, to share each other, to create special memories, will all combine to shape and grow them, even if it is only to love each other once. It remains special, a product of fate, a course meant to be, and there is nothing that the two lovers could ever do or say, which could alter it.

It is inevitable and unimaginable love.

Of course, Renee was always going to be Renee. That was part of her amazing charm.

We started to dress and to pack up before the mosquitoes arrived and they devoured us. I gathered my clothes and while doing so, I noticed that Renee was now doing the same. Despite the fact that her clothes had dried in the sunlight, when we hung them up after lunch on some nearby tree branches, she surprised me by asking for the whereabouts of my hockey warm-up pants and my Long Island Roosters tee shirt. I pulled them out of my hockey equipment bag and as I handed them to Renee, she began a typical Renee explanation.

"I will wear this stupid get-up home. Do not give me any bullshit about it! Technically, the tee shirt is hockey related, but I guess I have to support my boyfriend, who is also now my amazing lover, and support his employer a little bit too. Confession time. I am doing it for several reasons. First off, I will wear not one stitch of underwear underneath it. As your eyes keep telling me, I am still stark naked here, so I will tease you and keep you all hot and on edge all the way home. And don't you dare comment on my eyes following your glorious, huge, swinging male parts and your bare ass right now, because now, I am trying to gain some lost ground here."

She looked over at me to gauge my reaction and I somehow resisted bursting out laughing at her comments and description of my anatomy. Instead, I only smiled and listened to this marvelous woman. I knew the reasons for her speech, but there was no way in Hell that I would interrupt her.

Renee continued, "I have to have some element of power over you. Your power and love overwhelmed me. I feel so different. Extremely fulfilled. My body and soul are calm. Having you inside of me, so close, well, it settled me. I found perfect love. A perfect man and fit. After what you just did to my body and my soul, I have to make an admittedly vain effort to recapture the dominant side of this relationship. Second, it will cause my parent's some pause to know why I am wearing such silly clothes of yours and the circumstances behind how I ended up doing so. Of course, they will not ask and supposition will abound."

Renee posed a bit as I stood there admiring her naked body while she slowly dressed in my clothes.

"I am my own woman, you know."

"My mind and various, now swinging parts of me, have noticed and reacted to that fact, Renee. Yes, indeed, we have."

She smiled and said, "They have, eh? Ya parts reacted, eh? Oh yes, I noticed the reaction. Ya would have to be blind not to see it. Incredible reaction and astounding manhood. I don't how it all fit, but it sure felt amazing. Tomorrow might be hell between my legs, but it was still totally worth it. Yes, Paul, you are a smart ass. Astoundingly sexy, indescribably handsome. And I am quite sure that you are a lover with no equal. I say that, because you turned my world and body inside out and brought me to places that I never imagined today, but you still deep down, are a smart ass. A quiet and covert smart ass."

I shrugged my shoulders, pulled on my underwear and then my pants, paused and lifted one finger in the air while saying, "I might add that regarding your effort to be the dominant. . .."

Renee ran over to me, as she said, "Ah, ah, no, too slow on the draw. Your long-winded ass is too slow. Do not even go there. I have decided that you are a covert smart ass in disguise. Maybe you can tell the flavor of ice cream? Who knows with you? There seems to be no actual limit to what your power entails. There is no doubt that you are a smart ass, though. Yes, that is what you are."

"By the way, you ain't too shabby a lover yourself, there Renee," I commented. "Besides, ya look unbelievably hot wearing that rooster tee shirt."

She looked down at it, pulled it tightly over her bare breasts. The outline of her amazing breasts clearly displayed under the now tight shirt and she laughed and said, "Stupid ass logo!"

Then, quick as a flash, Renee changed in disposition.

"Last, although these clothes are freshly laundered, they still smell like you do, Paul."

She alluringly sauntered over to me and we embraced as she whispered in her husky voice tone, "Not too shabby a lover? Oh, no? Not too bad for a rookie?"

Renee lovingly placed her hands on both sides of my face and pulled me close to her as she told me, "Paul, the only way for me to survive now, is that I need to keep you close by my heart all the time. I require a daily dose of Paul. Paul, we are magnetic. Magnetic. My skin smells just as you do from our endless love-making. Your smell is distinctive and powerful and full of manly scents. I will hate to wash the smell out of these clothes. Perhaps, I will always keep them, forever, for me always to recall what we are, and all that we have shared."

We finished dressing, packed up the jeep, and made the long journey home. It was during the ride home that I noticed a profound change within my lover. Renee was now very different. She was strong, quiet, relaxed, and, for lack of any other description, fulfilled. Her usual snarky attitude and language, she packed away for a time. She held my arm gently, and she spoke softly and calmly. During the ride home, we discussed every subject that I think we have ever discussed; (except for our love-making) we covered trout, the sunset, the jeep, her education, my full-time job and what our plans were for next week.

She even asked me when my next hockey game or practice was! Now, I knew that things were a bit different. In fairness, and to clarify that statement, Renee did not say she planned to attend any hockey related activities; this was just a gentle inquiry into what the schedule was.

All too soon, the long ride was over.

I pulled the jeep into her driveway and jumped out. Before I could reach the other side of the jeep, Renee already appeared at the rear of the jeep. She was not the type of gal who always allowed you to open doors for her.

She, at times, needed to broadcast her assertiveness.

"I think it is best if we pile the fishing gear, fly rods, and everything else here, right next to the garage door. I will take care of it from here."

She looked up towards the sky and I could see her smile widely. It was a fantastic night, cool and crisp, with a sky that was crystal clear. The stars were out as well as a bit of the moon.

"Yes, more than three stars are up there. Shabbat is ovah. They have spoken their Havdalah, but still, there is no actual sense to you meeting my parents now."

I looked at her, a bit puzzled, and asked, "Are you sure? I feel terrible for not helping you with the gear, or meeting your parents if you wanted me to. I am ready, but if you are not comfortable with what happened today. . .."

Before I could even complete the sentence, she forcibly grabbed me, put both of her hands firmly on both cheeks of my backside, pulled me close, made me lean down to meet her, and she kissed me deeply.

Afterwards, she whispered, "I am more than comfortable, and I truly hope that both of my parents just witnessed that kiss and my grip on your gorgeous ass. Lutheran and Jewish, my ass. I am and always will be, my own woman. I just feel that it is too late and would be too dramatic right now. I am not ashamed of anything, mostly I am not ashamed to say that I have fallen hopelessly in love with you and I have absolutely no regrets of having shared every inch of our bodies and every ounce of my love for you."

Renee, despite her height, gently reached up, pushed my head away from her face, and she stared deeply into my eyes.

She then rather forcibly asked, "More importantly, do you have any regrets, Paul John Henson?"

Now it was my turn. I gently tilted her head forward and kissed her forehead while speaking just above a whisper, "No regrets. None. My grandfather taught me a long time ago that regrets are for fools. Regrets are only foolish doubts of decisions that we made. They serve no purpose. They only cause us angst and worry. Make a choice, be a man, then move on. Never doubt."

"Your English grandfather told you that?"

"Yes. I never met my other grandfather. He passed away just before I was born."

"Your grandfather is a very wise man. You are very lucky to have such a rabbi."

"I am lucky, yes in many ways, and he is."

Renee buried her head into my chest and we held onto each other in silence for a few minutes. I could hear her softly breathing. I pulled her tightly into my chest as she sighed deeply. Underneath the tee shirt, I could feel her bare breasts lift and heave against my chest. She pulled in so tightly; it was as if we were one.

She finally spoke, gently, softly, "Please, call me in the morning. Please call me around eight. I will be up very early and I will answer. I promise, Paul. Always know that I will always answer. As I said, I would love to love you once. Now, I will love you forever. Until the end of all time."

We parted with goodnights, a last kiss, and the words of my grandfather echoing within my heart and within my mind. The entire ride in my jeep back to my house, all that I could think of, was how deeply in love I now was, and there were just a few words which would not stop echoing within my mind.

"Never doubt."

Chapter 4

Forever, I Will Still See Her Eyes

I called Renee on the telephone promptly at eight the next morning. True to her word, she answered on the second ring. We spoke on the telephone for over two hours. Before I met Renee, I had only ever spoken with Maureen on the telephone for more than fifteen minutes. I was not a big fan of long telephone conversations.

The truth was that we could have spoken for ten hours and not run out of subjects. We hung up with a promise to speak on Tuesday of the upcoming week. I had some hockey commitments and Renee had university classes on Monday, so Tuesday worked best for both of us. Renee told me that she would call me early in the evening on Tuesday and we could make some plans.

For the first time in a long time, I felt as if for just a moment, hockey left the primary position within my heart, and perhaps, now just perhaps, someone or something, had overtaken it for the primary position.

Maybe.

I thought it strange at first, when the telephone never rang on Tuesday in the early evening and I found myself standing and staring at it quite often, almost willing it to ring. More than once, I resisted the temptation to pick the telephone up and dial Renee's number. I filled with apprehension at that task, preferring to think that Renee needed to dial me first, unless we had made prior arrangements. I would never want to place her in an awkward situation with her parents.

Tuesday almost slipped by until the telephone rang late. It was almost ten o'clock when the old man summoned me to the telephone. I had heard it ring; I was sitting up half-asleep in my bed, pensively reflecting and willing the ring on the phone. This entire day had a bad vibe to it; my connection to Renee was strong and profound. I could tell that something was wrong—something was seriously disturbed and greatly unsettled.

"Ya better come get this call quickly, Paulie. It is that gal, Renee, and she does not sound so swift," my father said as he waved me over to the telephone.

I jumped out of bed, hustled over to the telephone, picked it up and instantly asked, "Renee? What is going on? What is wrong?"

"Oh, Paul. Oh, Paul . . . it is my father!" Renee stopped speaking and all that I could hear were quiet sobs and Renee gasping for air between them.

My stomach turned, and I felt my throat closing up. "Renee, please, my darling, Renee. I am here. What is it?"

Renee recovered, and the words came out just above a whisper, "My father . . . he is gone. Oh, Paul, you are my beloved. I have to tell you that he is gone. Can you come here, quickly? I need you. I need your immense strength and your quiet power because I have lost all of mine."

I felt my heart sink and my head spin. I did not have an effective reaction. It was too overwhelming now.

"Of course. I can come over, of course. . .."

When I returned home early in the next morning, my father was, as he often was throughout my youth and beyond, waiting up for me. He sat in his easy chair in the living room and he looked up at me as I walked in the front door and passed through the living room. It would not be many more years that would pass, and I would leave our family home at 182 Belmont Avenue to strike out on my professional hockey career.

Except for occasional visits, I would never return.

I would end up traveling the nation, but I have, in many ways, now come to realize that I never actually traveled much farther than that living room there in that old home.

"Did her father pass away, Paulie?" My father asked me as he motioned for me to sit.

I sank down on the sofa.

"Yeah, yeah, yeah, he did, Dad. He keeled over at work, suddenly, at his desk in his office. A massive heart attack. They could not save him. Poor man worked day and night. A big job, a big executive guy. Stress aged him before his time, Dad."

"Shit . . . that is too bad. I've seen it before. Some of the big shots who run the shop. The big boys who sit up in the fancy offices above where the shop is. One or two of them have keeled over too, ya know, over the years, they croak. Overwork and stress, kills ya. They all have funny looks in their eyes, like all they think about is work, production, money and success."

My father looked at me and then down at the floor. He was searching for some words and when he found them, he leaned back in his chair and asked, "What the hell is success, really, when ya think 'bout it?"

"I dunno, Dad. After tonight . . . I just dunno."

"I will tell ya what it is and where it lies. Ya cannot count success or measure it, Paulie. I think what really counts in this life all comes to you from within your own heart. That is where happiness and the true measures of success lie. You know, you can be the richest man in the graveyard."

I looked at my father, and despite the intense pain of this evening, I smiled. He had such profound statements, and in many ways, I could only wish to be as smart as he was.

"They are Jewish folks?"

"Yeah, yeah, yeah, Renee, she is Jewish. The family is very religious and strict but Renee, not so much. She beats her own drum."

"And Renee is from a wealthy family?"

"Yes. Very. They have a beautiful house."

"Is that a big problem? I have to say that is not exactly the greatest mix ya know. Bet ya can get some older folks mighty upset, ya know, raise a few eyebrows. A poor boy from the old, rough neighborhood. A Lutheran boy, long-ass blonde hair, a beard with blonde and red highlights, tall, muscular, and handsome. Ya know, messin' with some rich Jewish gal. Besides, the history there does not work out too well, ya know."

"I know that, Dad. I understand and dunno. I can only tell you what I feel. She is very special."

The old man did not answer me. Instead, he studied me for a long time. I studied him too, looking to tap into his wisdom.

"She's pretty too, huh?"

"Dad, yeah, yeah, yeah. Well, you have no idea. Beyond pretty. Astounding."

"Oh, I do, Paulie. I do. I can tell by the way that you have been in the last few months. Love don't follow no rules. Nuthin' wrong wid that. You care for her deeply, I can tell. Plus, ya can't ever fool your mum. She looks in your eyes for the clues. Don't ever play poker for a shit load of money or be a secret agent. They both would be some of the few things in this world that you would fail at."

"People have told me that too, Dad. They really have."

The old man smiled and said, "Mum . . . she knew the first day that you talked about her. She said you were in love with her."

I did not answer him.

I did not have to.

"Ya sure, ya not just in love with her beauty? There is

more to love than just a few awesome rolls in the old sack. There is more to it than just how beautiful a woman is. Show me the world's most beautiful woman, and I will show ya a man who is sick of makin' love to her. Not every woman is like ya mum is where she gets prettier and smarter every day! It could be that . . . well, ya know her looks might fade someday. Ya got to be careful, ya a very good-lookin' guy too. Be careful that youse guys are not just lookin' in mirrors and that ya are lookin' inside of ya hearts too. Looks fade, hair turns grey, breasts sag, bellies and backsides get fatter and softer. Love is not what ya see in a mirror, it is what ya feel inside of ya hearts."

People who dismissed my old man as being just a street tough guy from New Jersey did not know the true soul of a very brilliant man, with endless knowledge in his mind and deep feelings in his heart.

More life lessons.

"No, Dad. It is so much more than just that with us. I understand what you mean and I appreciate the advice. I really do. This is not just skin-deep. It is a connection, deep, solid and profound. We talk for hours and hours, and our conversations send shivers up and down my spine. Renee is not like any other woman who I have ever met. Ever."

The old man nodded, and he smiled again.

"Gotcha. I know the feeling. Ya mum and I, well you get it. Well, geez . . . it is a rough time, a terrible, terrible time, so make sure to support her now, Paulie. You love her. Help her out. You have a quiet power and strength that people take from in times of need. In these times, you will be her strength. I have to say that there ain't nuthin' ya are afraid of in this world."

The old man leaned back in his chair and he sighed.

"For some strange reason, we all tap your strength, Paulie. It is who you are. I cannot explain it. Ya got it from Gramps. Your emotions are controlled, but strong. You have immense power. My best advice is for you to get some sleep. Ya need a recharge."

I nodded my head in agreement.

"I think them Jewish funerals will be right away. Isn't that, right? As long as it is not Showbotty or whatever they call Friday?"

"Shabbat, Dad. Yes, the funeral is tomorrow."

"Make sure you wear that black suit and tie your tie knot straight. You always screw it up. Damn, wonder how you will get that hockey puck thing on your head with all of that hair. Oh well, tie your necktie like I taught you. As far as the hockey puck on your head, you are on your own for that one."

"I will, thanks, Dad. For everything."

It was the first Jewish funeral that I ever attended. I did not know it at the time that later in my life as a clergyman; I would attend many Jewish funerals and many other Jewish events. I sat in the facility's rear, quietly, with a kippah on top of all of my hair.

Renee and her mom, and some other people, whom I guessed to be her grandparents, and perhaps some aunts and uncles, all sat in the same row. Her mom was as beautiful as Renee was.

The family sat in front of the room, near the casket. I could see her, and it might be hard to explain, but I could not truly *see* her. Instead, and perhaps more profoundly, I could feel her. And for now, that would have to suffice. Although we were not actually physically sitting together, there remained that ever-present connection within our hearts. She saw me; she sensed me, and then we briefly spotted each other for a moment, when Renee turned around and scanned the crowd behind her. It was then that our eyes met and our love burned into each other's souls.

Once our eyes met, then we solidified our connection. She knew that I was there to love and support her, she could lean upon my strength, and that was all we required.

Most of the service was in Hebrew, but occasionally, the

rabbi in charge shifted to English and I could certainly follow the Old Testament words, some Psalms, excerpts from Lamentations and some of the prayers. Mostly, I could tell that I was sitting with other non-Jewish folks, a mixture of Christians, Protestants, Catholics; they all chimed in about when I did so whenever we recognized some type of common liturgy. These people, I surmised, were mostly coworkers and neighbors of Mr. Gorman; they certainly were as much as a fish out of water as what I was!

After the service, in a receiving line, I briefly met and spoke with Renee's mother for the first time. On the evening of the day, when her father died, when I went to meet Renee, Mrs. Gorman was in mourning with her sister, and I never met her. I only sat with Renee in her living room and comforted her for many hours, so this was our first actual meeting.

What a horrible moment for a first meeting with your girlfriend's mother!

Mrs. Gorman, as I mentioned, was beautiful. She was taller than her daughter was, but only by an inch or thereabouts. You could see her striking features, of which she passed on to Renee. She did not speak. She only nodded her head, but she stared deeply into my eyes for what seemed to be more than just a few seconds. I thought that was very strange how she deeply studied me.

I only whispered, "Friend of Renee, Paul John Henson . . . is my name. I am so deeply sorry for your loss," and I moved on.

I did finally meet with Renee; she embraced me warmly and individually and carefully kissed each of my cheeks as I did hers in return.

She could barely speak, but she whispered to me quickly, "Thank you for being here. I do love you, Paul, with all my heart and soul. Please, come sit Shiva with us. It will be a wonderful mitzvah for you to visit and sit with us. Do you know about sitting Shiva?"

She checked my face for my reaction as I nodded affirmatively. I was vaguely aware of the practice. Our neighborhood was quite diverse, and I had sat Shiva with Mum and my sister once, when a Jewish neighbor passed away a few years ago.

"I will be there. I know not to speak, unless one of the mourners speaks to me, although I would not know what to say. I also will not greet you."

She weakly smiled and gripped my hand tightly and said, "Not true. I mean the part about you not knowing what to say. You always know what to say, Paul John Henson. That is part of your quiet magic. Thank you for you and all that you are. Here, forgive me, but you can sew this later. You need to have a Keriah . . . here, over your heart. I should have done this before the service, with the rabbi, but I don't play by the rules. I want you to wear it, as if you are part of my family and a direct mourner, not just a visitor. As you now know very well, I am a rule breaker, and very much my own woman."

She reached into my suit and gently tore the corner of my shirt pocket. Renee then turned, joined with her mother, and they continued to greet other persons in the receiving line.

After the services and burial, I returned home, changed my clothes, washed up, and then jumped in the jeep and rode over to the east side of the city of Paterson. I knew there were a number of kosher delicatessens and Jewish bakeries on the east side of the city. There was a large Jewish population on that side of Paterson, and I knew that would be where I could obtain some advice in order to purchase some baked goods or some type of pastries that would be appropriate to bring to the Gorman's household for sitting Shiva.

A kind woman with a heavy, yet traditional, New Jersey Jewish accent smiled and nodded her head as I gently explained my situation and asked her for advice of what would be a perfect gift to bring.

I did not want to blow this one; it meant too much to me. I had to admit for a man who could stand courageously in front of one hundred miles per hour hockey pucks hurtling towards my head without flinching; my nerves were on an edge about this visit.

In fact, I would go so far as to say, my knees were knocking too!

"I am sorry to hear of your girlfriend's loss. I have the perfect gift basket, right ovah here. It has some fruit, some desserts, some different types of bread, it is all you need and is reasonably priced too," the clerk said while she pointed and smiled. She then kidded with me a bit to cheer me up.

"My, my, my, she is a lucky Jewish girl, to have a handsome man such as you are, and, mind you . . . even before you told me, I could tell that you are not Jewish. My goodness, such a shame. I would marry you myself if you were a good Jewish boy!"

I laughed as best as I could. I appreciated her kind remarks and efforts to cheer me up. It was easy for me to take her sound advice; therefore, I paid her for the basket, thanked her and left with my confidence boosted just a bit.

It was time to head to the Gorman's house to sit Shiva.

I took Mum's advice and dressed once again in my suit. I still needed to wear the shirt with the torn pocket; therefore, I agreed with her statement, "Better to be overdressed, then underdressed, Paulie. Besides, it is not as if you have many choices."

Mum was correct, since my wardrobe was rather sparse.

Nervous did not accurately describe my disposition, it was actually that I was close to shaking in my shoes and nervous as nervous could be, when I approached the front door of the Gorman's house. The driveway and street were full of cars; therefore, I knew that the house would be full with many visitors and family too. I had to park my jeep all the way at the end of the street, which was a good location for me. It would give me time to walk and relax a bit, too. While I slowly walked to the Gorman's house, I worked on a plan to slip in and somehow become lost in the crowd. It would be hard to do when you are six feet five, have long blonde hair with tinges of red hanging down past your shoulders.

I slowly walked up to the front door and noticed that the door was open, so I gently knocked on the door, and when a man standing on the stairs inside the home waved me in, I opened it and walked in. Walking into the foyer of the home, I looked around and admired how wonderful it was. It was a large home, majestic and beautiful.

This was a typical split-level home, a very common type of home in this part of New Jersey. The split-level houses all had a staircase leading down to a lower level, with a staircase leading up to a living room and a kitchen directly in front of you at the top of the stairs.

The man who waved me in was silent. He glanced quickly at my torn pocket; in fact, he did a double take, but he did not comment. Instead, he pointed towards the kitchen when he saw the basket of food that I was carrying. Since I knew that the custom was to remain silent, unless spoken to, and to refrain from greeting any of the mourners, I simply nodded, walked up the stairs, and set the food down on a kitchen table that was already full of all types of food.

I mixed in quickly. It was very crowded, but even through the crowd; I could see Renee sitting on the floor of the living room, next to her mother and other mourners. She was dressed all in black, she wore only slippers upon her feet, she wore no makeup and for the first time in the time that I had known her, she had no jewelry on today.

Renee did not even wear her usual earrings.

There was a single candle burning, while sitting on the windowsill of the large picture window that faced the street in the living room, and I noticed a large mirror, covered in a brown paper, hanging on the wall at the top of the stairs. This was in accordance with the tradition of the mourners, not to be concerned with their appearance during the Shiva period of seven days.

I found this all quite fascinating and rather sensible too.

Perhaps my timing was perfect, because a few visitors came in right behind me, who were obviously Jewish, and they, too, set food down in the kitchen and then moved to the living room. I purposely stalled a bit in my approach so I could follow their practices and mimic what they did. They did not say a word, only a gentle glance towards the Gorman family, and they moved to a number of seats in the living room, where they sat down.

I followed behind the other visitors, did the same that they did, and tried hard to fit in. Both Renee and her mother looked at me, and I watched and then felt their eyes following me.

No one said a word, but as usual between us, Renee's eyes told our story.

Her eyes revealed to me that I could tell that she was, despite the terrible circumstances, quite appreciative of my visit. There were no open seats available. Therefore, I picked a corner of the living room and quietly sat down upon the floor. Renee was across from me, not directly opposite, but within direct sight. She remained expressionless, yet she looked at me frequently, but still no one spoke. We all sat in silence for quite a long time. It seemed as if hours had passed.

Perhaps they actually did. Honestly, I was not exactly sure, and I dared not to glance at my watch!

It surprised me when Mrs. Gorman suddenly looked up. She glanced towards an older chap seated very close to me and she asked him what his fondest memories of her husband were. The older chap immediately perked up, and he related stories of discussions they shared over drinking a few beers while sitting in the backyard of this home, speaking about his favorite interests of fishing and watching baseball games.

Based upon the direction and nature of their conversation, as well as his testimony, it was obvious that the chap was a neighbor, or perhaps a close friend.

The neighbor's words broke the silence in the room. It was as if his words broke the silence in the entire world. Mrs. Gorman thanked the man for his kindness and his memories. She then asked the same question of an older woman seated on a chair in the room. After the woman related her memories, Mrs. Gorman had the same reaction. Then she moved to another visitor, and then another.

I sat in silence, listening, taking it all in. And it was very easy to conclude that Mr. Gorman was an extraordinary man who had lived a remarkable life. The testimonies told the story—he was deeply loved, would be deeply missed, and he was a kind and good man.

He cared deeply about his family and his friends, too. I never met the man, but could tell that he was special.

After all, he helped to raise a remarkable daughter!

I was now relaxed and settled in, strangely, somehow; I was trying to enjoy the celebration of a special man's life while simultaneously mourning his loss, when I nearly jumped out of my skin when I heard the soft voice of Renee asking me what my memories of her father were!

From the experiences of my young lifetime of playing the position of goaltender in hockey, you would think the one lesson that I would have learned was never to relax. Never, ever relax.

The entire room turned towards me and awaited my answer.

Ah, geez!

All I wanted to do was to hide here in the corner and try very hard to blend. Why would Renee have asked me such a question? She, of course, knew that I never even met her father. Everyone was staring at me; I was on the hot seat now, when I suddenly recalled what Renee told me after the service, "Not true. You always know what to say, Paul John Henson."

Ah, no, I do not, and everyone is now staring at my torn pocket too. Okay, breathe and think, Henson! Think! Why did Renee do this to me?

My mind went blank until a dusty memory came into the deep recesses of my mind. My grandfather and his teaching of so many valuable things, from fighting for what you stood for, to standing up for your decisions, for being a tough guy when you had to be one, to being a fair and gentle man when that too, was required.

Lessons of life, which were invaluable.

Another invaluable gift that my grandfather had given to me was the love of books and reading. He shared his love of reading with me, and in many ways inspired and encouraged me to write on my own, to put down on paper, in words, some of my own thoughts, adventures, and to tell these stories of ordinary life.

Well, perhaps, in retrospect, they are not quite fitting too well into the ordinary category.

Gramps had given me all the classics to read since I was old enough to read, and I enjoyed them all. When I was very young, I was already an advanced reader, easily reading and comprehending books and materials, well above what should have been my normal reading level.

Cover-to-cover, I read them all, many times over, books, novels, short stories, from all the brilliant authors, Kipling, Conan Doyle, Stevenson, Melville, Dickens, and many others. In addition to those classics, Gramps also gave me a copy of a Bible.

In addition to my own Bible studies and religious

readings, my family attended our Lutheran worship services together most every weekend. I was a Sunday school student for a long, long time, but most of what I knew about the Bible came from my reading it cover-to-cover. Many times, over, in fact.

At this point in my young life, I was not yet a Bible scholar, but I had a fabulous memory and I was a voracious reader. I never dreamed at that time how all of that Bible reading would help me later in my life, or how it would spark a flame inside of me that burned brighter and brighter while my life went on.

Suddenly, I knew what to say. A verse came into my head. Old Testament, Paulie, be sure to stay away from any of the New Testament. C'mon, twenty-seven, do not blow it now! My mind whirled around; I needed to recall that the Hebrew names for the Old Testament chapters were different. Think, think, think. My self-studies paid off, because it all came back to me now.

I cleared my throat and spoke softly, "Well, his love of fly-fishing, his love of the outdoors, with clear rivers and pristine trout streams, brings to mind a verse from the Books of the Writings. Ketuvim. All streams flow into the sea, yet the sea is never too full. To the place where all streams come from, there, they will all eventually return."

Looking up, I glanced around the room and met Renee's eyes. For the first time in this horrible, two-day period, they did not have tears in the corners of them. The remarkable sparkle had returned.

I finished by saying, "That is what comes into my mind. I think what this verse is actually saying, is that our circle of life never really ends. It all returns over and over again. It goes on forever, for all of us, now and until the end of all time. I think we always return to one another. We never really leave our loved ones, not ever, and they do not leave us."

Renee went to speak, but Mrs. Gorman gently touched

her daughter's arm to prevent her from speaking.

Mrs. Gorman did not smile, except with her eyes, and she looked at me while she gently spoke, in a voice just above a whisper, "Thank you so much. He so loved fishing in the streams and he so loved the outdoors and he did indeed share and pass that love off to Renee. That passage was so perfect. So beautiful, Mr. Henson. It is remarkable for you to recall such a verse from only your memory. It was simply beautiful."

The sparkle in both Renee and her mother's eyes told the entire story.

Thanks once again, Gramps!

After the intense and moving experience of sitting Shiva with Renee and her family, I developed a terrible sadness creeping in my heart, mind, and soul. It was as if I knew beforehand what the next days and weeks would result in. When Renee did not return my phone messages, or call me in the days and weeks after sitting Shiva, I knew what was unfolding in the Gorman household.

I was many things, but a fool was not one of them.

Now that Mr. Gorman had passed away, everything had changed. Our lives together would never be the same, and even my strongest wishes, prayers, desires, and dreams could not change the inevitable. I knew where this was going to end, and I agonizingly ran different scenarios through my mind to come up with some way to change it, to alter what I knew deep in my heart was now going to be the end.

When the call finally came from Renee, I knew what she would say, in between a rain of tears and halting words, even before she said it. I knew what the plan would be, and I told Renee that I would help in any way that I could.

Supporting Renee and Mrs. Gorman in their time of grief and sorrow was paramount to me, but that did not mean that I was ready to accept or believe what Renee told me the plan now was. I felt as if the destiny of our meeting and our intense love was for a profound reason, and despite the tragic circumstances, what I felt was our unavoidable love being brought to an abrupt conclusion was just too harsh and entirely too devastating.

After our intense conversation, many sleepless nights ensued, tossing and turning in my mind because I knew there must be more to it than this.

Renee had held back on the telephone and it was obvious that she needed to tell me the entire story in person and not on the telephone.

It was a gorgeous, warm, clear August afternoon. It was unusually pleasant for this time of the year in New Jersey, as if it was a foretelling of an early autumn arrival. No humidity, no thunderstorms building in the late afternoon. A perfect day, except for the reason that we were gathering at the Gorman house.

I leaned upon the fender of the jeep, quietly watching the moving crew move the remaining last pieces of the furniture, boxes and possessions of the Gorman household into the moving truck parked in front of their home. My eyes studied the "for sale" sign from a local realtor that now stood in the yard, out near the edge of the street. It proclaimed the status of the Gorman's house in red, blocky letters.

Renee stood next to me, gripping my hand tightly. Her eyes filled with tears. She was quiet, pensive, and reserved.

As the last pieces of their lives in New Jersey were loaded into the moving truck, she turned towards me, looked up and asked, "Paul, would you please come and unscrew the Mezuzah from the front doorway for me? I removed all the others, but I am too short to reach the one in the front."

She handed me a screwdriver and took my hand as I nodded. She seemed not to want to let go of my hand. She took it and squeezed it tightly at every opportunity that she had. We walked hand-in-hand in silence to the front door, where I took the screwdriver and carefully unscrewed the Mezuzah from the frame.

I handed it to Renee, who very softly and quietly whispered a gentle, "Thank you." I watched her first kiss her fingers to her lips and then touch the Mezuzah with her fingers before she placed it in her pocket. She spoke some words in Hebrew, but I did not understand much of anything of the words. Then again, I might have caught a few words, enough to realize that it was a prayer, something about comfort.

After we were finished removing the Mezuzah, Renee once again took my hand, and she led me back down to the base of the driveway where Mrs. Gorman met us.

Mrs. Gorman spoke softly and gently, and she too had remnants of tears displayed in her eyes, "I want to thank you again, Mr. Henson, for your invaluable assistance. Here are all the keys to the home. The realtor called earlier and said that she would meet you here by four in the afternoon. I hope that she does not hold you up. I know that you have a hockey game this evening out on the island."

I took the keys from her hands and said, "It is no trouble at all, Mrs. Gorman. My pleasure. I will make sure the keys go into the realtor's lockbox and that I have the code. The house will sell quickly because it is a majestic home."

She nodded as I saw her eyes quickly glance towards the home. Tears rimmed along the edges of her eyes.

"I will check the house as often as I am able to. Harry and I are out here at the ice rink all the time anyhow, so it is not any trouble. We will cut the grass, maintain the property as required, and fix anything that we find damaged or troublesome. To a certain extent, Harry and I, well, we can repair most anything."

Mrs. Gorman's eyes lifted and without hesitation, she asked, "Even broken hearts, Mr. Henson? I believe to a certain extent that is within your abilities too. That will be an invaluable ability for you to possess for the next few months, or perhaps even longer."

I did not answer her, but upon hearing the words, Renee squeezed my hand even tighter. Mrs. Gorman came closer, and she placed her hand gently on my arm, then she reached for my other hand and gently grasped it while her daughter held the other one.

"You are an exceptional young man, Mr. Henson." Her eyes widened for a moment, and she studied me quickly before speaking again.

"My goodness, you are such a large and imposing young man. Your presence is captivating. You are physically imposing, yet you are thoughtful and gentle in your mannerisms and in your approach to life. I can tell that you are extraordinary in many ways. You're a hard worker, determined, proud, a young man who is wise beyond your years, who has learned that you work hard for what you earn both in wealth, spirits and in love. Your parents and grandparents raised a special man. You are a credit to them. Now, it is very true that we do not have very much in common. In fact, we are worlds apart in our cultures, upbringing and in religious beliefs, but that does not much matter with a person such as you are. Your eyes tell of your kindness, Mr. Henson, but they also are a beacon of your strength. I would say that a person should never interpret any of your kindness for some type of weakness. I fear that might be a very grave error on their part."

Renee now relaxed her grip on my hand and she leaned into me. She let go of my hand and she wrapped her arm around my waist.

Her strength was now gone.

Renee needed me to support her and for me to lend her some of my own strength. I did the same, and pulled her in tightly, while still holding Mrs. Gorman's hand.

Mrs. Gorman held back the tears while she pensively

looked away, she studied the house again, the yard for a few moments, then she spoke once more, "My Renee, she is strong, powerful, she is outspoken and very much her own woman. Only a very strong man could tame her, love her, and understand her. You are strong, tall, powerful, both inside and out, and handsome to perfection, Mr. Henson, yet fearless to a fault. Shortly after you both met, I noticed the change in my Renee. It is none of my business, and I would never ask or pry. You are both adults, but I know what you have shared. I do not judge . . . but I am her mother. My dear Renee, she is now calmer, gentler, lovingly fulfilled. She is a woman who now knows strength and love shared with a strong and wonderful man, perhaps her equal. Indeed, perhaps, he is even stronger than she might be. Yet, he is a man who is quiet, caring, loving, and calm. All of those things are gifts from you, to my . . . no. That is an incorrect word. My apologies. They are gifts to *our* Renee. Remarkable gifts that HaShem gave to you, Mr. Henson. Thank you for sharing them with our precious Renee and with the world, Mr. Henson. Never hold them back, for they are part of HaShem's plan for you."

I did not know how to answer her; once again, my mind was blank, so instead, I gently squeezed her hand, until the words came.

"You are very kind. Thank you for the generous words, but I am sure that I do not deserve them. All I can ever do is the best that I can do. Nothing more and nothing less."

She let go of my hand, leaned in, and warmly embraced me, while speaking in Hebrew, or Yiddish, I did not follow the words at all.

She then leaned back, placed her hands gently upon my cheeks and said, "Oh, yes you do, Mr. Henson. You more than deserve them. I will leave you two alone now. This will be an extremely difficult moment for you and Renee. My sister is waiting as well as the moving crew requires my signature. My heart goes with you, Mr. Henson. No, no, no—my heart goes with you, Paul. After all, who can say what our futures will be? Perhaps that stream you mentioned when we were sitting, Shiva, will flow back to the sea someday and bring all of us together. That is my hope, and that is my prayer for you and my daughter. B'ezrat HaShem."

She looked at me, gently touched my cheek with her hand, while I told her, "I will keep you in my thoughts and prayers, Mrs. Gorman."

"As will I, Paul. Shalom, Kol Tuv."

"And also to you."

Mrs. Gorman turned and walked away in the direction of the moving van, over to where her sister was standing on the sidewalk waiting for her. I heard Renee sigh deeply, and then she exhaled. I knew that this was going to be more than difficult; it was going to be unbearable. Renee once more grabbed my hand, and this time, she pulled and tugged me along and led me to the other side of the jeep.

She was rather forceful and determined and while she directed me, she said, "Please, over here, Paul. This is going to suck enough, but to have an audience watching us might be more than I can stand."

We walked over to the other side of the jeep, and in front of the passenger's door, she stopped, gently turned into me, and buried her head into my chest.

I heard her softly say, "Damn, you are so friggin' tall. How I wish that I could easily reach those lips." Renee was trying hard to break the tension and remain strong. It did not work.

She then sobbed. I could instantly feel her tears upon my tee shirt.

I held her neck softly while she sobbed and I spoke quietly, "Shhh. . . c'mon Renee, it is going to be okay. I am here and I will always be here. I might become a dusty, old memory for you, but on your darkest days, you will always be able to recall your fondest memories."

She cried for a little while longer, and I gently held her and we rocked back and forth for a time. She finally looked up, and I wiped the tears away, first under her right eye, then under her left eye.

Renee seemed to gain some composure, she was too powerful to fall completely to pieces, and she spoke, "I think . . . no, no, no . . . I am wrong because I wanted to believe that I could somehow change my ways. I did not think, in fact, I knew in my heart that this day would arrive someday. I just did not want to face it, or admit it, or think that it would arrive as quickly as it has arrived. Yes, not under these horrible circumstances and perhaps not this soon, but it had to arrive."

While gently cupping her head in my hands, I told her, "You know, Renee, it does not have to be this way. It is not quite clear to me and I do not entirely understand because I can go out to Colorado and join you. There are hockey clubs out there. Number twenty-seven just has to play out the contract here, find a team and have a try-out with them. Goalies are always in demand. I hope that you know that I would gladly go to Hell and back for you. I am actually not afraid of. . .."

She reached up, removed my hands away from her head and held them tightly in her hands.

"No, Paul. I know that you would die for me and I would die for you. That is not in question. Following me to wherever you see, my love, that would not work. I am going to tell you why in a minute, but first, you need to understand that I am not breaking off this relationship. I am releasing you because of how much I love you. How much I care for you and because it is the right thing to do for you. The trouble with our love and our relationship is that on the surface, to everyone else looking in, it is all wrong. Yet, in our hearts and in our souls, it is so right, so perfect, and so flawless. It is perfect. That is why the pain of all of this always will remain inside of me and perhaps, you too. I think our religions would have been a horrible obstacle, my father . . . well, let's just say that it would have been very difficult to say the least. However, the biggest trouble would have been me."

"You, Renee?"

"Yes, me. I would, or could, never share you. I love you too deeply, too intensely, and way too powerfully. You are a dream and you need to realize that you become an actual part of a woman who falls in love with you. You invade her inner soul. That is how your power has enveloped me. Yet, I am too controlling, too possessive, too jealous, and eventually, your love of hockey and your career dreams would drive a wedge into me. I could never share you with anything or anyone. Well, perhaps, with one other person. I could share you with our child, or with our children. They would be a part of you and a part of me. Part of our love. Yes, Paul, I would share you with our children. Otherwise, I would be terribly possessive and horribly jealous. I am too selfish. You are way too precious to share with anything, and hockey has invaded your soul, Paul."

I now had the answers in which I was seeking. In my heart, I knew there was so much more to this, and now Renee had confirmed my instincts.

She looked up at me as if to gauge my reaction and confirm what she already knew, and that was the fact that I would never lie to her and try to say that hockey was not a huge part of my life. Renee smiled gently, her eyes filling with tears, her emotions overwhelming her. But I did not let her down.

Never would I, on purpose, disappoint her.

In an odd sort of way, it confirmed our love for each other, in that we would never lie to each other just to pacify the other's feelings. We were too genuine with our love.

I did not answer her, because I had no reply, nor did I have a rebuttal. She was correct. My dream was to do exactly what I was doing right now, and this pattern seemed to repeat during my romantic encounters. Maureen had told me almost the identical thing. Yet, I could not help but to feel this incredible pain in my heart, and to some extent, feeling some burden of guilt, of being in love with this wonderful woman and trying to fulfill my dreams, too.

"Paul, if it were not hockey, then it would be another career dream of yours that you would commit your heart and soul to. As my mother just said, you are an exceptional worker, dedicated and sincere to your mission. It is how your parents and grandfather taught you, to always give your best effort to anything that you make a commitment to do."

I smiled and nodded while pulling her in tightly to me for a moment. This is why we were such magnetic lovers right from the start, because we knew each other so well.

Renee spoke quietly, while she rested her head upon my chest as our arms remained wrapped around each other's bodies, "How, I hoped and even prayed that there was something that I might have, which I knew would allow me to possess you for my own. If I was pregnant with your child, then I knew that would be the bond that we needed. However, a week or so after we were together, that dream ended."

Renee now pulled away from me and faced me while taking my hands in hers. Her eyes were dark and serious; the sparkle had left for a moment, the sparkle now chased away by raw emotion and tears.

She whispered, yet spoke the whisper of words confidently, "I know the answer already because of your honor, but I still need you to tell me that if I was carrying your child that you would give it all up for us. Tell me that, Paul . . . would you have married me, despite all the other obstacles?"

I recalled that special day, a time long ago, when I was just a young boy. I once again recalled that afternoon when I learned a powerful lesson or two from Gramps and my father in the Widow's Pub. Not the least of, was that you work hard, earn what you work hard for, and always stand for what you believe in. Backing down from what is right or true was not part of my genes.

Life's lessons come at you hard, but they stay with you forever.

I let go of her hands, gently pulled her head up, held her by the chin, and kissed her deeply. When the kiss was over, I whispered, "In a second."

She smiled, buried her head into my chest again and answered, "It would take me less than that to say, yes."

We held each other again for a long time and spoke nothing at all; we just held each other and rocked gently back and forth.

Renee finally broke the silence.

She studied my face and eyes and our eyes remained locked on to each other as she spoke, "I guess, despite how badly this all sucks, you do understand. After Father passed, there is nothing left here for us. We have to go back home, regroup, restart, and I have to support Mother. My aunt, she knows about pain, she lost my uncle and she came out here to stay with us. Now, we can all go and be with family and it makes this logical, an excuse to end this here and now. A clean break, to end what my jealousy would have eventually ended, anyway. It was inevitable. Hockey or not, or whatever you end up doing with your life, HaShem has marvelous plans for you, Paul. Your nature is to share all of your kindness and strength with others, and to make commitments to your work, to what you believe in and whom it is that you love in this world. It is how HaShem guides you, Paul. Mother knows, she is wise to the ways of HaShem, and everyone who knows you can feel that, sees that, understands that fact. I just wish that it included me in those marvelous plans. I could not even share you with HaShem. I would need you all to myself because you are so rare and so precious."

"I love you dearly, Renee, and I understand. I really do, that is, because of how much I love you."

"I love you too, Paul John Henson. I will now, and forever. There is no doubt that I will love you until the end of all time. There forever more will be Renee and Paul. Our love and relationship will always exist in some way and somehow."

Renee looked up at me and her face had changed a bit from an appearance of anguish to a radiant glow. It was as if she was now accepting in her heart and soul the fact that our love would transcend time and always be a part of our lives.

She gently reached up and cupped her hands on the side of my face and she spoke again, "No matter whom I might love in my life, there will always be a special place for you in my heart. You will always be my beloved, my greatest joy, and my greatest love. I am not ashamed to say that now, and I will say it forever more. Time will never diminish that love. Goodbyes are the effing worst, so let's end this now, a kiss and one last word, which of course, will have to be mine."

I thought for a brief second that Renee almost laughed, and when I went to say something, she reached up and put her hand over my mouth. She was not going to allow me to say anything.

"Quiet. Please, my glorious lover. Please do not speak. I want the last thing that I ever heard from your lips to be what you just said, that you love me and that you understand. That is all you have to say."

I honored her request and pulled her tightly into my chest as she exhaled. I could feel her breasts lift and heave against my chest. She pulled in so tightly; it was as if we were one.

"I need to smell you, Paul. As I once told you on that glorious day, you have such a distinctive smell. I will never forget it. I wish I could bottle it, unscrew the cap and have a dose of you whenever I wanted it. I swear the last vision that I will ever have before I die, will be of you. I swear that it will be, no matter where I am, or who I am with, when I take my last gasps—I will see you. Now, say nothing more, please just one last kiss and I will turn and leave. I will not look back. I cannot, because it will kill me. Please, and you will not chase me down."

I had one last look into those incredible eyes, one last look, which needed to last an entire lifetime.

Despite the pain and urges to change all of this, how Renee had requested this to end, was exactly how it happened.

We kissed long and deep. I finally let go of her, and so far in my young life, it was the most difficult thing that I ever had to do, in order to let go of her hand and watch her walk away. I could hear her sobs; I could absorb her pain and I could feel her love.

Inevitable love brought to a heart-wrenching conclusion.

I plodded to the driver's side of the jeep, watched as Mrs. Gorman, Renee's aunt, and then finally Renee, climbed into their car. Mrs. Gorman started the engine, and they drove away.

The moving truck followed them and I remained there, watching until their taillights disappeared around a corner. I did not even move my feet, nor lift my eyes from the view of the road, until I could no longer hear the engines of the vehicles or the rumble of the tires upon the asphalt of the street. Long after their vehicle was gone, I remained leaning upon the fender of my jeep, staring down the street, hoping, dreaming, wishing. . ..

I never saw or heard from Renee Gorman ever again. Never a letter, nor any telephone calls, or even a card.

I also never sought her out or tried to find her.

I often thought about how Renee had said, "Always know that I will always answer. As I said, I would love to love you once. Now, I will love you forever," and those words haunted me, day and night.

There were many lonely nights filled with haunted dreams.

A few times, shortly after Renee left, I had the urge to try to seek her out, find a telephone number and call her because I was positive that she would, as she told me, "Always answer."

Just one of the countless special and sincere aspects of Renee Gorman was that she did not mince words, or ever say anything that she did not mean.

I resisted the urge. It was heart wrenching, but it would have been wrong to perpetuate the anguish of the situation. I felt that I would, instead, rest upon the memory of our love and tuck it away deep in my mind for safekeeping. We both knew in our hearts that this scenario was the only way that it could ever be, because anything else would have been even more painful to endure. As if this was not painful enough to even try to think about, let alone endure.

About four hours or thereabouts, after that horrible and heart-wrenching goodbye, the Long Island Roosters hockey club, and a certain goalie for the Roosters named Paul John Henson, played a game out on Long Island at our home arena. I played exceptionally well in the goal that evening. Perhaps it was the pain in my heart coming out in my play, I do not know. I was on fire, aggressive, almost combative in the net, and I played the game with an energy of which I was not too sure of where it had come from.

To me, there was little doubt that it was one of the best games that I had ever played.

The next night, I went back to The Gaslight Lounge for the last time. Gary the waiter asked me if Renee would join me, and he and the rest of the wait staff sensed my sadness, when I softly mumbled that she would not be joining me tonight. I sat in our corner, at our table and poked at a dinner, while drinking much more than I usually did or should have.

Sometimes, you just need to numb the pain.

Maybe the old bloke, Davison from the Widow's Pub so long ago, was wrong about many things, but tonight, I shared a bond with him; it was just over many different circumstances.

The wait staff felt my pain. They left me alone and when the time came for closing, Gary came over and he put his arm around me and said to me, "C'mon along now, twenty-seven. Time to go home, big guy. Do you have a game to play tomorrow?"

I shook my head to indicate no.

"Please give me the keys to the jeep. It is going to be okay. I feel your pain. Renee was amazing and while I do not know the details, I do know that she loves you no matter whatever happens."

I looked up at Gary out of shipwrecked eyes as he pulled me up out of the chair.

Doing my best to muster up a smile, I told him, "I know that, Gary, and that is why I needed to drown her memory for just a few hours. How I wish the power of our love could stop the sun from setting and prevent this day from ending. Yet, she will return in a few hours, when all of this liquid courage wears away. Then, I will do my best to banish her forever from my mind, but she will never leave my heart."

The little waiter shook my hand and said, "I am so sorry, twenty-seven. Look, you need to rest. Come along. Damn. Good thing you do not have a game tomorrow. Your ass is goin' to be hurtin'. I wish I had an answer for you, but I have no doubt, twenty-seven, that you will remain in her heart too."

Gary gently took my keys to the jeep. He led me to a waiting taxicab that he had very wisely called for me. He had even called Harry to make sure that he could bring me back the next morning, to pick up my jeep.

Everyone in the world knew the world-famous Harry M.

Redmond Junior!

The staff and Gary had made the correct decision because I was not in any condition to drive. He also was correct in his prediction that I would be hurting the next day. I felt worse than if I took ten slap shots dead on in the mask.

My head was a wreck.

Harry understood about the situation. He quietly and softly quizzed me the next day, while we drove to pick up the jeep, but he did not probe. He knew, of course, the fact that Mr. Gorman passed away suddenly, and I think he put the pieces together from there on in, as to the fact that Renee had left New Jersey and returned home to Colorado. I think that he knew, in that special kind of Harry way, that this particular situation, for many reasons, was extremely painful, but I wanted to keep the details of my relationship with Renee to myself. Harry respected that fact, and he knew that if and when I wanted to talk about it, then he would be there for me.

He always was there for me and me for him.

Looking back, I found it quite profound that the only thing that I really recall about the ride back to the restaurant to pick up my jeep was something that Harry said to me.

At one point during our mostly silent ride, Harry reached over and he gently put his arm around me while saying, "Ain't none of my business, twenty-seven. I can tell ya wanna keep it to yaself for now. I will be here for ya when and if ya need me. I am sure that ya already know that. If ya don't wanna talk 'bout it, I understand. Just wanna say, she might have broken your heart, but ain't no one or nuthin' in this entire world, who can ever break number twenty-seven's spirit. Your spirit is still alive and above all, ya still are the world-famous number, twenty-seven. Powerful and fearless. Ya always will be."

I do think those words might have sustained me.

After Harry drove me the next day to the parking lot to pick up the jeep, I never went back to, or even considered going to, The Gaslight Lounge . . . ever.

My parents steered clear of the subject of Renee Gorman, too. I could feel them studying me carefully in the weeks following the departure of Renee. Yet, they never said a word or asked me any questions, and even without any sort of expression of my feelings, I appreciated their concern, but also appreciated their respect for my privacy too.

The fact of the matter was that I knew what was coming next. It was a pattern in my life that was to become all too familiar. Now, it was time for the ghosts to arrive, to haunt me, to burn into my soul.

She was gone. Yet forever and forever, I will still see her eyes.

Chapter 5

Grassroots Are the Best Roots of All

I must say that this particular cup of coffee might have been the best coffee that I had ever had. I am primarily a tea drinker, but there were times when a cup of tea just would not cut through the excessive haziness of my mind and get the job done.

This was one of those times.

I came back to reality and shook off the haziness of those dusty old memories. I looked around and the sun was now much higher in the sky. The last remnants of the coffee in my cup were cold, and the drifting of my mind had only allowed time to escape me once again.

Most of all, this daydream was now over, because the ghosts of the past, which seem to always haunt me, floated away.

All I had lost was a little more time, but perhaps this time, while being haunted by these incessant ghosts, I had also regained something. Something that I needed to recapture once again. A part of me that I always had and I never actually lost, but for some reason, until recently, I had not used. Perhaps, on this quiet day, lost in trout streams, tumbling rapids, and dusty, old memories of extraordinary love, I had regained parts of my spirit.

It had been a remarkable day, and looking around at the river in front of me, I realized that this was just about the same stretch of water of which Renee and I ventured into so long ago.

In fact, maybe this rock was the very rock.

I could not be sure.

Even all of these years later, I still had never even shared with Harry the in-depth details of what I had shared with Renee Gorman. That fact, in itself, remains very unusual. Harry and I shared just about everything back then, and even now, we still do. I still find my lack of sharing any mention of Renee Gorman, or even conveying vague details about how deep and powerful a relationship that Renee and I shared, to be very interesting. It was as if my relationship with Renee was too sacred to share, even with Harry.

In looking back at all of it, I think that only Mum really knew how much we were in love.

I banished the memory of our relationship so deeply, so secreted within my soul, that it was as if I wanted her memory to never surface ever again. I was wrong and foolish to do so, because inevitably Renee returned. I think our love was too strong and powerful for it not to return someday. It was inevitable, and now it was time to face it and admit it.

However, even after all of these years, I stuck to my roots, to my teachings, and I have no regrets of the love which we shared, and I have little doubt that somewhere down deep, we both still share. Regrets are for fools. Regrets are only foolish doubts of decisions that we made. They serve no purpose. They only cause us angst and worry. Make a choice, be a man, then move on. Never doubt.

My goodness! These were such powerful memories, vivid, all consuming. And perhaps I should have picked a different location to resume my pursuit of fishing. Then again, maybe this was the correct spot to choose to return to an activity that I had been away from for way too long.

Perhaps I invoked these memories on my own, a special message from deep within my brain to revisit this place, in an effort to recapture parts of me which I might have lost along the way.

I had been praying for a long time for guidance, for direction, to assure myself that I was following the plan, to understand why I had these nagging thoughts as of late about Renee. This restart of sorts might just be the answer to those prayers, a ticket to change me, and provide me with new insight.

Relight the flame that was burning too low.

It could be that first, I needed to recall certain aspects of my life, in order to sort them out, or selectively purge some of them from within me. On the other hand, perhaps, it was in order to recall a special time, with a very special person, to put the events into perspective with where I now was in my life, career, and my marriage.

Reaching deep inside of you, to admit self-truths is one of the hardest exercises to do, to admit truths or guilt that you share only with yourself and with God.

I am not too sure, but subliminally, I might have chosen this location to fish on purpose. A deliberate choice, in order to remind myself that despite my intense love for my wife and family, in order to move on with the next phase in my life, I had to have the courage to admit that I knew exactly what it was that Renee, and I shared here.

Here in this very special spot, we shared and honored our love so long ago and it was, without a doubt, very special. I needed to acknowledge that our love was deep and powerful, yet it was all in the past. I needed to reconcile the fact that in my life, yes, I have loved two women with all of my heart and all of my soul, and there is nothing wrong with that fact. However, the fact of the matter is that one of these women, I married, is the mother of my children and I am spending my life with her. The other woman, I did not marry, and as tragic it as it might be, I had to admit what Renee already knew so long ago, that at that point in time, I never could have married her. In this wild path of life, of which I had chosen, I have learned that until you taste the bitter edge of your life, then you will never appreciate the sweet aspects of it all. I needed to understand that the relationship between Renee and me, no matter how intense and special it was, or might still in some strange manner still be, has no relevance on where I am now in my marriage, or how much I love my wife.

I needed to close the door on my past. Moreover, perhaps, it was finally the time to set Renee free from me, and me, from her.

"Hey there, young fellow! How goes the luck today?"

I nearly fell in the river when I heard the strong voice call out from behind me. I turned around to see an elderly man standing on the riverbank. He was dressed to the hilt for fishing. He stood there wearing hip waders, wearing a fishing vest that was equipped with a wide assortment of dry flies hanging on the pockets, flaps and folds of the vest. On his head, he wore a hat with numerous dry flies and nymphs hanging upon it, and he had a fancy, seven-foot fly rod tucked under his arm. He carried a creel around his waist and a trout net hung from his belt. He was a picture-perfect fly fisherman!

"Oh my, I must confess, your voice made me jump here. In all previous times that I have fished here, I never ran into another person fishing. I guess that I did not expect to see anyone."

"My sincere apologies for scaring the shit outta ya, there young fellow. I kinda snuck up on your ass. Blindsided ya! I saw you jump out of your waders! I have been fishing here for many years and I have to say, you just might be the first fellow fisherman that I have run into here too.

Quite strange indeed."

He walked over closer to me and I stood up, tossed the lukewarm coffee into the river and capped the top of the thermos with the cup. I put out my hand, as did the fisherman, and we warmly shook hands.

"David W. Washington is the name and fly-fishing is the game. Just what ya needed, some damn stupid-ass cliché. Huh? At least fishing is my game, when my wife tells me that I can go fishing, and ever since I retired too. Fifty-two damn years, I worked in a dye factory. I guess I earned a day or two on the trout stream!"

"I'll say you did! Paul John Henson is the name here. It is my pleasure to meet you, David."

"Nice to meet you too, Paul."

He waved his hands in the air quickly as if to encompass my face while he commented, "Lots of hair and beards, and stuff going on there! So, any luck?"

"Oh, I did well. Earlier, that is. I am one or two away from my limit. I caught all of them on nymphs. Brookies and one rainbow."

"Nice. I think there might be a hatch on the stream soon. I think that I will use dry flies. Do you mind if I give it a go here? It was not my intention to take your river."

I laughed a bit and waved towards him. I had to confess that I had taken a long break to daydream.

"No, no, no, please do. I must admit to sitting upon this rock for a long time while drinking coffee and I think that I became lost in it all. I have not actually been fishing for a bit, in fact, I have lost track of time."

"That is what fishing is for. Fishing is to lose track of time, Paul."

I watched as David finished his statement, and then he eased out into the river and flipped his fly line out from his rod. A few gentle waves, several back casts, more line, more line, and then he cast a gentle roll of line into the deep pool of water in front of him.

He was an expert fly-caster, not unlike that same gorgeous gal of so long ago was. . ..

His eyes and my eyes, together, followed the fly as it tumbled and floated through the rapids. There were no hits, no rises, nor strikes, and when the fly finally drifted towards the shore, he peeled the line in and repeated the motions over again.

After four or five casts with no hits, strikes or rises, he tucked the rod under his arm, reached in his vest pocket and pulled out a pipe. I watched as he packed some tobacco into the pipe and worked hard to get it perfect for a smoke.

"You have to leave just a little loose tobacco at the top, Paul. If you don't, it burns too hot."

I chuckled and shouted out from my position on the rock, "I will take your word for it. I never smoked. Pipes, cigarettes, cigars, or otherwise!"

"Ya, better off, but a pipe or two will not hurt you. Ya gonna join me? C'mon and float a nymph above me and I will cast over here. There is lots of room here on this river to share, and half of the fun is just floating the fly. The mystery of what lurks below is the other part of the fun."

I smiled and waved, put my thermos into my gear bag and grabbed my fly rod.

"Sure, David. I will join you. Thank you."

I waded out carefully into the river, into a comfortable location, about ten feet north of where David was casting his line, and the two of us began to float flies through the pools and rapids. My plan would be to stick with my nymphs while David floated dry flies up on top of the water. After a few casts without any rises or strikes, he pulled a different fly from out of his hat, removed the fly that he had been using, and tied the new one on. I stuck with the same pattern as a nymph, which brought me earlier success.

Between puffs on his pipe, he asked me, "So, Paul, what

do you do for a living? You do shift work, or are you goofing off today to allow you to fish during the day on a weekday?"

"In the grand scheme of things, I guess I am goofing off, David. Actually, I should be at work. I am a Lutheran pastor."

His head spun around quickly, and he stopped his arm motion in the middle of a back cast and lowered his fly rod to his side. I was used to the same reaction whenever I told anyone what I did for a living; it was almost as bad as when I told anyone years ago that I was a professional ice hockey goaltender. You know, the long hair, the beard, the hippie appearance, the rock-and-roll tee shirts and canvas sneakers. One thing that I was not, in addition to not being a fool, was that I was not stereotypical!

"No kidding, I would have never guessed that to be what you did. Ya sure are a hairy guy for a clergyman! My apologies for the foul language that I was using, but I had no idea you were a man of God."

I completed a cast and my eyes were following the nymph down through a deep pool, but with my free hand, I waved in his direction and shouted out above the sound of the tumbling water, "No apologies required. I do not fit the mold, I know that, but the real shocker is that I am, and always will be a pastor, but right now, my official position is that I am actually the bishop for this district of our Lutheran synod."

"Oh my! I am fishing with a bishop! One of the big guns! Now, I know we will catch some good ones! Can you whip up a prayer or two for trout fishing success there, Bishop Henson?"

"Please call me, Pastor Paul. I never became used to, or comfortable with, the entire bishop title. You know David, I will try a prayer or two, but I think God is fairly busy these days and not actually watching trout streams! Despite my profession, I am just a man. I am not special, nor am I virtuous. I still need the blood of the cross and I kneel before God and confess my humanity, just as everyone else does. We all fall and I have fallen short many times. I am human, just as Jesus was human too, after all, Jesus wept."

David nodded at my words, and he picked his rod back up and started to cast his fly. In the chilly morning air, you could see the puffs of smoke emitting from the bowl of his pipe. He was deep in thought.

Fishing provokes that from within you.

He finally spoke, as we both continued to cast, "Forgive me, Pastor Paul, but you are a humble son of a bitch, aren't you? Most bishops or clergymen that I have met want to make other people small because they think they are above the clouds. Do you know what I mean? I guess you can tell that I am not much of a churchgoing man."

David stopped short with his words. He suddenly pulled back on his rod and shouted, "DAMN! Did you see that, Pastor Paul? A nice brownie came up and looked at my fly, but did not strike. I guess that I have to change it to a darker pattern."

I had not been looking, but instead, I was watching my own leader as it floated through the pools.

However, I was listening, and I commented as such, "No, David. I missed that. I am not sure I have the angle to see it, anyway. Yes, sure, I think that I would tie another fly on there. As far as not being a churchgoing man, well, I think I disagree. I can tell that you believe in God because you are out here in this cathedral of his creation."

I waved my free arm over the river and stretched my arm out to encompass the entire area.

"You are sharing in the beauty of all of this; therefore, this is your church, David."

Once again, he tucked his fly rod under his arm and plucked a fly from his hat. He put the leader in his teeth, and bit the old fly off, and tied the new one on. I could tell that he was pondering my comments.

Finally, he spoke, "I like you, Pastor Paul. Damn, honest bastard ya are. You are grassroots, and grassroots are the best roots. They dig in the deepest in this life, and ain't afraid of doing it to survive. Ya tell it as it is, and looking at the size of you, I imagine there are not too many people who would disagree with you either. I think you are correct. I do believe in God, and this is a church, a religion of sorts. So, you are saying that church can be anywhere that you choose it to be?"

"Anywhere, David. Where your heart is and God is present, right here in this trout stream, you are honoring the glorious creation and the majesty of the beauty of it all."

He laughed, began a long back cast, and then said, "This is a handy piece of information to have. Now, instead of telling my wife I am going fishing, I will tell her that I am going to church! In thinking about it, I deserve it. All the years that I put in at that horrible factory. You know, I could have worked for another three years. That damn factory offered me to stay for fifty-five friggin' years, but I told them, no. For what? A lousy fifty extra bucks a month! I will eat pasta instead of steak, cuz I don't have the fifty bucks, but I gave them enough of my life, inhaled enough of their shitty chemicals and damn, I intend to fish and enjoy the time, which I have left."

David waved in the air with his free hand as he spoke, "Ain't no use in being the richest man in the graveyard, Pastor Paul."

The words he spoke sent ripples of shock cascading up and down my spine. I clearly heard my father saying the same words on the night in which Mr. Gorman passed away. Another lesson that my father taught me long ago, a lesson that I ignored or had forgotten, and now that I was older, his wisdom, as well as my grandfather's wisdom came back to me again, as it had time after time within my life.

It all became clear, and while it was not money, of which I sought that drove me to work so hard, it was instead a weakness of my character to try to find myself and please people by proving myself, over and over. It was a byproduct of the demands of playing the position of goalie in professional hockey, where even one goal that you allowed is never good enough. You have to work harder and harder and be flawless. Well, I am flawed, and it was time to stop trying to prove to everyone that I was not.

All I can ever do is the best that I can do. Nothing more and nothing less.

I now knew why my former boss and predecessor, and unbeknownst to me until recently, my mentor, Bishop Von Houten, played so much golf. After his many, many years in the trenches, he had nothing left to prove, and he did not give a damn, or care to answer to any person who felt as if he still did.

Another lesson learned.

I am not ashamed to admit that I care for that man with all of my heart and soul as he does me. When I first applied to the ministry, Bishop Von Houten was the one person outside of my circle of family and friends who believed in me when very few people took me seriously.

He gave me the chance of which no one else would, and I will forever be in debt to him for his faith. We were, and still are, very close.

I had come here today looking for someone that I left behind a very long time ago, and I not only found Renee and admitted the extent of our love, and assured myself that I still had no regrets, but I also found the pieces of myself that I left behind too. It was time to collect them and to make myself whole again.

My stream had made it to the ocean and returned, and it was now time to jump back into the waters and begin the circle of life again. Who knows where God will allow the waters to bring me to this time around?

We fished in silence for a long time; I received no additional strikes. David caught one small rainbow trout and lost that same brown trout, after it this time, took his fly, but the fish shook the fly loose in the midst of a long battle.

I suddenly had an idea, a thought to bring this full circle.

"David, it has been my pleasure, but I think I will pack up my nymphs for today. I still have two more trout waiting for me and I know where to find them."

"Oh yeah, okay, well nice meeting you, chatting with you, and I hope to see you again soon. Say, what is your idea?"

"Perhaps, you would know for sure. Does the river still switch over to allowing bait farther on downstream? That is how the rules were years ago, but as I had said, it has been a long time since I fished here."

David watched as I waded to the riverbank. He tucked his rod under his arm and waded over to me with his other arm and hand outstretched.

We gently shook hands, exchanged some additional parting remarks, and he said, while pointing downstream, "Sure, sure, sure, good idea. You will knock them dead with a worm or two. It still switches to bait, down there, right about where the river bends and curls."

I thanked him, smiled at his perfect choice of words, and walked to gather up my gear and head for my jeep. He waved goodbye and thanked me. For what he was thanking me for—I was not sure; it was his words and wisdom that I needed more than he needed mine.

I scrambled up the steep bank. More ghosts and memories swirled around me while I did so, but this time, I tried hard to ignore them. I made my way to the jeep and packed away the fly rod and flies, and instead, I grabbed my trusty old fishing pole.

The pole that I also knew for all these many years as my collector's item.

I also grabbed out of the jeep, a small package of worms that I had purchased at the bait and tackle shop late yesterday, just in case.

Back down to the stream, I baited the hook with a worm on the end of the line of the old pole. I set my sights for my cast on a curling section in the swift rapids of water, right before the stream moved into deeper and slower water. After picking the location, I gently tilted back and snapped open the bail of the reel. I performed a gentle cast into the water and the cast effortlessly landed and then rolled the worm into the rapids. The worm disappeared in the water's foam; it floated amongst the rapids for a few feet and then . . . BOOM! I set the hook hard and watched in delight as a good-sized rainbow trout took the worm and tried hard to dig underneath some nearby rocks. The fish was no match for the old pole; the reel was still smooth and spun without effort, and after allowing the fish to run a bit and enjoying the fight, I pulled it onto shore and netted it.

I admired the colors, the beauty, and when the fish recovered from the fight, I set it free once more. I watched the trout scoot off into the depths of the deep water. The trout was free once again, and I could relate to that feeling too.

I also felt free once again.

Another cast, then another, and BOOM!

Success once again, and this magnificent day was over.

I returned to my roots, to my beginnings, to the grassroots of my life, and David was correct. Grassroots are the best roots, they dig in the deepest in this life, and ain't afraid of doing it to survive.

I waded in close to the bank, found a rock, grabbed my thermos, and poured the last of my coffee into the lid. It was late now; the sun was thinking of the end of it all for another day, and it was time for me to head home.

Home to a restart.

Home to taking every Friday off from work, just as all

the pastors who worked for me did. Perhaps, every Friday, Binky and I will have a date night, or some family outings, and even a little fishing. I might just even take up golf! Bishop Von Houten would faint if he ever heard me say that.

On the other hand, even take a holiday or a long trip, maybe up to Canada, to visit my old hockey coach. Yes indeed, Coach Davis was always inviting me up to Ontario Province to fish with him; it might be just the time to do so. Binky would love to meet him, sightsee, and hike in the mountains.

Whatever it was that we chose to do, it was long overdue just to do it! Ain't no use in being the richest man in the graveyard.

I could not wait to return home, wash up, give my dear wife a long kiss and take her to some fancy restaurant for a night on the town. Maybe some dining and dancing too. Afterwards, well. . ..

A deep breath, a glance at the sunset, and an admiration of the majesty of the day sinking into the trees, a smile, and I knew that I was back.

Shalom, Kol Tuv.

In the end, it was all so simple, all so easy to find what I was missing and to face my own self-truths; I just had to have the courage to venture a little bit farther, to the very special spot where the river bends and curls.

THE END

Epilogue

"Shit, I do not think so. Geez, pal, that is an old song. I know we played it a long time ago, but it might be a little rough for the boys and me to pull it off tonight. Plus, this joint here is fancy. Some of these old geezers might not appreciate that kind of music. Ya know . . . it is out of their comfort zone. They want to slow dance and hear this dull, lazy shit. We are so sick of it, but it pays the bills."

I stood next to the stage, speaking with the leader and main vocalist of a band, which was playing at a fancy dining and dancing restaurant that I had taken Binky to on this Friday evening.

We had shared a wonderful, romantic dinner, as well as more than just a few drinks. Binky had enjoyed a few more than her usual number of martinis, shaken not stirred, of course, and I did not care. Tonight, it does not matter. There was a rented limousine sitting outside the restaurant to take us back home, so tonight, it was no holds barred! Now that the band was playing, a few couples had slow-danced to exactly the type of music that the bandleader described in perfect detail.

That music would not work for me, or for us. Not tonight, at least. I needed to rewind a very special memory from our past.

So far, this had been a wonderful evening; however, there was one piece of the puzzle that I required to top it all off.

Suddenly, another memory, another ghost, floated above me. This one was just the one that I needed to haunt me right now!

This was, after all, New Jersey, and it was time to take a page out of the world-famous Harry M. Redmond Junior's playbook. I reached into my wallet, found a crisp, one-hundred-dollar bill, and pulled it out. I waved it in the air in front of the bandleader and the drummer who sat at his drum kit and was watching the scene unfold, picked up his drumsticks and played a quick drum roll.

While quickly drumming a few beats on his skins, he shouted out to his boss, "I think that piece of music just came back to me!"

The bandleader smiled, took the one-hundred-dollar bill. He placed it in his pocket and said, "Okay, pal. You got it. Please give us a few minutes to sort it all out. We have to find our Spanish horns setting on the electronic keyboard. These old bags ain't gonna be happy though."

I shook his hand and said, "Deal! You are on the payroll now, pal. They will get over it! Believe me, when I tell you that I have done this before. Soon, they will all be out here shaking their asses and having a grand old time. You just said you are sick of playing that music, anyway."

I turned and walked back to the table where Binky had been watching the scene unfold. I think she knew what was coming, and as I reached the table, I bowed in front of her and extended my hand as an invitation. She reached for my hand and smiled while she stood up.

It felt as if the entire restaurant was watching us. How could they not watch? Sure, we were older, but Binky was still the most gorgeous woman on the face of God's good Earth.

She could take a man's breath away.

She was dressed to the hilt, diamond earrings, a golden necklace, wearing a tight, black dress with a plunging neckline, displaying her marvelous cleavage and amazing and still captivating female figure. She was and will always be a goddess. No man in the entire joint could take his eyes off her.

We walked hand-in-hand slowly out to the dance floor and Binky leaned in and said, "Paul, it has been so long. I do not think I remember the steps. Plus, your knee, as of late, has been sore. My back is tricky. I don't think we can pull it off. After all, we are not twenty years old any longer."

I grabbed her, spun her, and held her tightly while giving her a passionate kiss right there in front of the entire restaurant.

In a gentle whisper, right next to my wife's ear, I told her, "Sure, we can pull it off. It is just like ice-skating, or bicycle riding, fishing, or sex. Once ya do it, ya never forget."

She laughed and softly said, "Living Love, huh? It has been forever since I have heard this song. I swear that I do not know what has come over you as of late, number twenty-seven. However, I do think, when we get home tonight, that you had better be ready to, as you used to say in your hockey days, to buckle your mask straps up tight. I might just wear you out!" She winked and smiled at me and then continued, "Okay. You lead, of course."

The bandleader was babbling into the microphone about a change in the musical program, a special request . . . yeah, yeah, yeah, sure, sure, sure, I have heard this all before. Get to the music, pal.

The unique Spanish influenced opening bars of the song began and I smiled, Binky squared off to me, smiled, fluffed her hair, and cast a sex appeal felt all the way back up the Garden State Parkway in good old Sussex County. In fact, a little earth tremor back home may have knocked over my mum's teacups.

I swept in and held her as the tempo of the song built up. I spun her at just the right moment, and we faced each other off at the end of a spin with almost perfect timing. Soon we were whirling, twirling, and shaking. Binky followed my lead, as I was loose and feeling the flow. I was in the net making the saves and feeling the game. The old goaltender moves were serving me well! It was pure magic to a purely magical song. As the song came down to the last bars of the tune, I pulled Binky in close, held her, and then spun her for a final clasp and a dramatic, perfectly timed ending. It surely helped that I knew every beat of that song. Thank you once again to the composer of this song. Wherever you were, you sure wrote a good one!

What Binky and I did not realize was the size of the audience that we had attracted during our dance. When the song had ended, the entire restaurant and even the kitchen staff, who had come out to see what was going on, all stood up and gave us a loud round of applause.

It was something special, and I must say, a scene that we had shared a time or two before.

The band broke into another song by the Electronic Transistor Orchestra, and what seemed as if it were the entire population of the restaurant, rushed out onto the dance floor, wiggling, shaking, and jumping to the music. They all dashed out there, uninhibited.

Old geezers, cooks, a waitress or two, a waiter, the bouncer even left his post to wiggle around, and even a maintenance man who had been changing a light bulb came down off his ladder and he danced too.

Yes, I have seen this scene before too. . ..

As we walked back to return to our table, our server came over, placed another round of drinks on the table, and smiled warmly and proudly at us.

"These are on the house from the manager. That was fantastic, youse guys! You must be professional dancers."

"Thank you, but we are not professional dancers. We just love each other. A lot."

I grabbed Binky and pulled her tightly into my chest as she sighed deeply. I could feel her wonderful breasts lift and heave against my chest. She pulled in so tightly; it was as if we were one. She, once again, sighed deeply and profoundly. Our love reinforced and unified.

We stood there in front of the table, holding onto each

other and rocking gently to the song.

While we gently rocked together, I prayed silently over and over in my mind, and thanked God for all he has given to me and that he continues to give to me. I thanked God for the love of this wonderful woman, for our children and for all we have shared and all that we continue to share.

I knew in my heart that this was a rare and precious woman that I was lucky enough to be holding in my arms. A woman that I loved more than anything else in this entire world. A woman with whom I shared a profound connection with now and forever until the end of all time. I knew that this evening, not only was it our words and thoughts that were in perfect unison, but that later on this evening, after we prove our love once again for hours and hours, and lay exhausted in each other's arms, that our hearts will beat together in a perfect rhythm.

Yes, indeed, in this crazy ride, we all call life; I can assure you that even on your darkest days, you will always be able to recall your fondest memories.

ABOUT THE AUTHOR

Way back in time, when the dinosaurs first died off, at the ripe old age of sixteen, Paul John Hausleben wrote three stories for a creative writing class in high school. Enrolled in a vocational school, and immersed in trade courses and apprenticeship, left little time for writing ventures, but PJH wrote three exceptional and entertaining stories. Paul John Hausleben's stories caught the eye of two English teachers in the college-preparatory academic programs, and they pulled the author out of his basic courses and plopped him in advanced English and writing courses. One of the English teachers had immense faith in Paul's talents, and she took PJH's stories, helped him brush them up, and submitted them to a periodical for publication. To PJH's astonishment, the periodical published all three of the stories and sent him a royalty check for fifty dollars and . . . that was it. PJH did not write anymore because life got in his way. Fast forward to 2009 and while living on the road in Atlanta, Georgia (and struggling to communicate with the locals who did not speak New Jersey) for his full-time job, PJH took a part-time job writing music reviews for a progressive rock website, and that gig caused the writing bug to bite PJH once more. He recalled those old stories and found the old manuscripts hiding in a dusty box. After some doodling around with them, PJH decided to revisit them. Two stories became the nucleus for the anthology now known as *The Time Bomb in The Cupboard and Other Adventures of Harry and Paul.* The other story became the anchor story for the collection known as *The Christmas Tree and Other Christmas Stories, Tales for a Christmas Evening.* Now, many years and over thirty-five published works later, along with countless blogs and other work, PJH continues to write. Where and when it stops, only the author really knows.

On the other hand, does he really know?

If you ask Paul John Hausleben, he will tell you that he is not an author, he is just a storyteller. His mission is to continue to write and tell stories to warm your heart, make you laugh, and sometimes make you cry, just a little. Most of all, he deals in memories, and helps you to remember the good times of your own life, and the special people who touched you along the way. Paul was born and raised in Paterson, and then nearby Haledon, New Jersey, and began writing at an early age. He revisited a writing career later in his life, and he now is the author of a number of novels, compilations, short stories and audio and video works. Most of his work touches upon nostalgic remembrances of simpler times, and tells the stories of heartfelt, humorous, and special human relationships. Other than writing, among many careers both paid and unpaid, he is a former semi-professional hockey goaltender, a music fan and music reviewer, an avid sports fan, photographer and amateur radio operator. He now resides in Somewhere, U.S.A., but his heart always remains along Belmont Avenue in good old Paterson, and Haledon, New Jersey.

Other Work by Mr. Paul John Hausleben

The Time Bomb in The Cupboard and Other Adventures of Harry and Paul

The Night Always Comes, Another story from the Adventures of Harry and Paul

Reunion, A sequel to the Night Always Comes and Another story from the Adventures of Harry and Paul

The Miracle Tree, Another story from the Adventures of Harry and Paul

The Chronicles of Henson

Heaven's Gain
The Final Adventure of Harry and Paul

Geyer Street Gardens
Beneath the Mask of a Hockey Goaltender
Another story from the Adventures of Harry and Paul

Crows on a High Wire

And a few others too!

Coming soon?
Stay tuned!

Paul John Hausleben

You may write to the author at ctte27@gmail.com

Published by God Bless the Keg Publishing
Somewhere, U.S.A.

This edition of *Where the River Bend and Curls* published with written permission of the author and in conjunction with God Bless the Keg Publishing LLC

Henrico, Virginia, U.S.A.
You may write to the publisher at
godblessthekegpublishing@gmail.com

"Life's simple pleasures are so often the best ones!"

Follow Paul John Hausleben on Facebook and enjoy samples of his photography, receive updates on new releases, and enjoy his general meanderings

www.ingramcontent.com/pod-product-compliance
Lightning Source LLC
LaVergne TN
LVHW010915110826
845149LV00013B/2372
9780990697916